A Tale of Two Homes

A Tale of Two Homes

by

Dr. V. Srinivas

White Falcon Publishing
www.whitefalconpublishing.com

A Tale of Two Homes
Dr. V. Srinivas

www.whitefalconpublishing.com

First Edition, 2017

ISBN - 978-93-86210-96-8

DISCLAIMER

Although Raven's Nest Homestay does exist, the characters, sequence of events, legal maneuverings and court cases mentioned in this novel are all fictional and purely a figment of the author's vivid imagination. If they resemble any person living or dead, it is purely coincidental.

"It was the best of times, it was the worst of times"

... A Tale of Two Cities by Charles Dickens, 1859

"Building a home far away, while current home breaks away"

... A Tale of Two Homes by Dr. V. Srinivas, 2017

Synopsis

This is a fictional narrative based on events at two ends of the spectrum:

(a) Living in Mumbai and trying to build a house in the Nilgiris
(b) Facing the prospect of the house one is living in being demolished

People without any experience in house construction would be considered foolish to try and build a house in the mountains thousand kilometers from where they live.

People living in a building which has been earmarked for demolition would be on an emotional roller coaster ride as the tension of not having a roof over one's head is unimaginable.

This story intertwines the two events with anecdotes and flashbacks.

The practical difficulties and adventures of buying the land, choosing an appropriate name, deciding on what to do with the property and finally building the house is one side of the coin, while the legal tangles, web of intrigue, mental stress that is unique to a high profile building demolition is the other side.

These two aspects form the basis of this story which does not follow the principles of "textbook creative writing".

CONTENTS

READER'S COMMENTS

1. **Vera Schaal, Designer, Reutlingen, Germany**

   I did finish the book in record time!

   I found that it was very easy reading. It was at times very amusing but also informative in a clear way.

   The mix of RRR and RN were well chosen, sometimes humorous and always with precision.

   My opinion was: funny, clear and not too drawn out.

2. **Dr. Thilak, Ophthalmologist**

   Got hooked - extremely interesting and well written- I'm a fast reader - so I finished fast. I promise to buy several copies when it is published.

3. **Ms. Cama, Advertising consultant**

   It's a good documentation of how you went about building Raven's Nest. Nice light style, easy to read and I liked the back and forths. In terms of balance there is much more of Raven's nest and not so much RRR which I'm perfectly ok with.

4. **Mr Seshadri, MA, LLB, Retd,**

   At last I was able to read your interesting book. It is very informative and entertaining as I am aware of the RRR story from other sources. It made good reading.

RRR: Raiz Rayne Residency
RN: Raven's Nest

5. **Ms. Setupathi, Editor in a Publishing House**

   I finally found the time and mental space to read your manuscript. First off, I want to say you've done a wonderful job and displayed a lightness of touch that is most endearing and entertaining. The Raven's Nest sections are especially fun to read, while the RRR ones, being full of legal woes, were less compelling. But I understand that from your perspective, there's an element of comparing and contrasting.

6. **Dr. Rao, Cardiologist, USA**

   The juxtaposition of the 2 scenarios [the RRR and Raven's Nest Project] is interesting but not new. The reference to a pregnancy and ultimately birth was good.

   To me the events related to the Raven's Nest were of much greater interest than the ones related to the RRR. [But, this is a personal bias]

7. **Mrs. Cariappa, Home maker, Coorg**

   I was delighted to read the extract from your soon to be published book!

   Well done, doctor Saab. I enjoyed it thoroughly.

8. **Mr Do'canto, Entrepreneur, Berlin**

   Congratulations for writing the book. I just started today and found it very amusing. The index with medical language and alluding to a pregnancy is both personal but also inspiring.

   I really liked reading the beginning and am looking forward to read more.....(as I am on a train from Berlin to Hamburg).

   ....Just finished the book as we pulled into Hamburg! Excellent!

9. **Dr. Gupte, Emeritus Professor Anaesthesia**

I have read it all and it makes a very interesting humorous reading. It is really very readable and gets the reader interested right from the start and you have put it in a very simple but extremely readable style, great, congrats.

I hope you have your wife's permission to say so.!!!

Congrats, whoever reads it will feel like seeing the place, it will be automatic marketing for Ravens Nest.!!!

10. **Dr. Namrata MPH (Harvard), a Dr. doing NGO work in India**

I really enjoyed reading your book. It's not a book only on house building but on relationships. Most importantly, relationship from a successful man's perspective. The humour is the USP of the book. I can guarantee the book will sell and will have readers all across age groups.

I would give this a thumbs up and thank you for sharing your work. I would love to get an autographed copy and pre-order the book

11. **Dr. Rekha, Marketing Consultant** (after reading the first 30 pages)

You will not need any help marketing. It is very well written and humorous. Had a good laugh. Waiting for the remaining 200 pages.

RRR: Raiz Rayne Residency
RN: Raven's Nest

LOGO PAGE

www.ravensnest.in

Raven's nest

www.chaletmonami.com

CHALET MON AMI

PREFACE

ONE OF THE perks of running a homestay is that you get to interact with a wide range of people from different walks of life with varied interests.

Recently, a family of doctors from Tamil Nadu spent a few days in Raven's Nest and when we narrated some anecdotes of what had happened during the construction, they were very interested and strongly suggested that we put it down in print. Their argument was that such books are written only in the West and very little content is written about such experiences and adventures in India. So, at their behest we put pen to paper or finger to keyboard to create this story.

If we get kudos for this effort, then we will be happy to reveal the identity of this doctor family who were instrumental in inspiring and stimulating us to get down to work, but if we get brickbats they will remain anonymous like most characters in this book lest somebody decides to sue them for malpractice!

Introduction

I HAVE A CONFESSION to make.

Normally, a confession is made on one's deathbed or at the end of a project but here I am making it upfront.

'A Tale of Two Cities' by Charles Dickens was a masterpiece written by a literary icon. On the other hand, 'A Tale of Two Homes' is a mish-mash written by a literary novice!

I am a Cancer surgeon by profession whose expertise lies in cutting up people and then stitching them back together, so much so that I am the designated tailor at home. My wife, on the other hand, is a journalist teaching creative writing. Since she was up to her eyeballs with other commitments, I took it upon myself to write this book and hence a small bit of medical terminology has crept in.

As I have only written scientific articles and never attended a creative writing class nor know the ABC of how to format a story, plot, characters or avoid clichés, this may be labeled as a piece of junk by critics.

However, in spite of my confession, if you still decide to buy it, please do get your '*paisa vasool*' *(money's worth)* as my dear Gujarati friends will say, by at least reading the book and you have my permission to pass it on to your neighbor at a discount, marketing it as a literary masterpiece!

PART 1

CONCEPTION

I CAN ASSURE YOU *that nobody got pregnant, but an idea (**Raven's Nest Homestay**) was born and to understand this we've got to ask a few questions.*

Why?

One 'why' invariably gets a short answer, but three 'whys' get a story. Raven's Nest is based on three 'whys'!

Why the mountains? Why the name and why a homestay?

Let's go on a journey and see if we can answer these queries and hopefully, this whole puzzle will fall in place.

Chapter 1

Mountains Beckon

My wife, a high society lady, glued to her latest iPhone and I, a simple surgeon, who does not even possess a cell phone, live in a high rise building with a lovely sea view in central Mumbai. The wife wanted a second getaway home in Goa as all her friends partied there and she felt left out. I, on the other hand, argued that the weather in Goa was hot and humid, similar to that in Mumbai and one saw the same sea, so why spend so much money getting a place in Goa only to replicate what we now had in Mumbai. Stupid idea!

My scientific argument was that we needed a place in the mountains where the air is cooler, fresher and a definite change from polluted Mumbai. Although my submission had merit, do you think high society ladies listen? It is pointless for any husband to argue with their better half as they will have to accept defeat sooner or later. So having learnt my lesson several years ago, it was a case of 'shut up and agree' for me.

Influential friends were contacted, realtors were beckoned and the ball was set rolling to find a luxury home in Goa...and you guessed right, I had no input in this exercise. My only job was to fund the project and ask no questions lest I get banished to the dog house.

Several weeks later a site visit was arranged and I was politely told that I should stay in Mumbai and attend to my patients since the wife decreed that she could not be bothered allowing her cell phone to be used for my patients' calls. As I said earlier, I do not possess a cell phone and this shortcoming is not related to the fear of increased brain tumors with its use. Far from it!

The story of why I don't possess one dates *back to the 1990's when I worked in USA. Doctors had to carry beepers and cell phones 24x7 as we were expected to be at the beck and call of patients. The dictum in USA was that the 'Patient is the King'. Sounds very altruistic and you may think this is contrary to what is believed in India where the 'Doctor is the King'. But just wait a minute and listen to what I have to say and you may agree that it is better to let the 'Doctor be the King'!*

The first requirement for any doctor in USA is to obtain professional malpractice insurance and once you fork up a hefty sum, the insurance company invites you to a big fancy dinner. So we troop into this fabulous hotel, little realizing that our money has gone into this lavish dinner and after we are all seated and wined, the chief insurance honcho makes his speech. His opening statement is, "How many of you in this room have been sued?" I wasn't surprised to see several hands go up - since I had been warned that this is what US medicine is all about. Hold on, his next statement was a shocker, "There are only two types of doctors in this room - those who have been sued and the others who will eventually be sued!" That was unbelievable and he went even further, "Remember, treat every patient who walks into your consulting room as a potential lawsuit and deal with them accordingly." So now you know why there is hardly any personal rapport between patient and doctor in USA but in India, the doctor is looked upon as part of the family.

Thus, answering the ubiquitous cell phone in a jiffy was the first step in preventing a lawsuit even if it meant that you were fired at home for not being easily available. On returning to India, I felt that it was better to throw the cell phone out, not worry about patients getting annoyed but be readily accessible to the high command at home like a good Indian husband! So now you know that it is NOT 'no cell phone-no brain cancer' BUT it is 'no cell phone-no home firing'. By now you must have realized that there is some form of role reversal in this family wherein the lady rules and this will become more apparent as the journey unfolds.

The visit to Goa happened in May, at the height of summer and as you can well imagine, the weather was a terrible spoiler and this dented some of the enthusiasm for Goa. Although no lady admits they have made a miscalculation, I was just told that I should not be in any rush to raise funds for a second home in Goa. Basically, I was instructed to continue my normal life and not ask too many questions. This I faithfully obeyed!

A few months later, I received a call from the wife who happened to be visiting Dharmasala and in a very sweet tone she told me that the Himalayas were gorgeous, the weather was fantastic and maybe we should think of a second home there. Of course I did not have the guts to tell her, "I told you so," but I was thrilled with this change in her perception of acquiring a mountain home, although in my mind it would be the Nilgiris and not the Himalayas.

On her return, she informed her other lady friends of her wise decision and instructed me to now do the leg work to find a good Himalayan mountain location. After a little research, I realized that outsiders were not allowed to buy property in Himachal, Kashmir and additionally most of the Northern hill stations are not conveniently connected to Mumbai. After carefully laying out the ground work of where not to go, I steered the conversation to the Nilgiris and got the wife to make the final decision that we should buy property in the Nilgiris and nowhere else. Wow! This was a battle won by stealth as I had schooled in the Nilgiris and this is where I wanted to have our second home, but if I had opened my mouth earlier, I was sure as hell that I would have been ordered to shut up! So this is the long and short answer to **the first 'why'.**

Chapter 2

Naming Ceremony

Now let's look at **the second 'why'** - the name Raven's Nest. Some people may ask, "What's in a name?" But in this case, **all** is in the name.

My lady and I have two lovely daughters who are diametrically opposite in temperament; one is a hippy and the other a yuppie. The hippy one studied in USA, grew dreadlocks in her hair, used to walk around in un-ironed clothes and felt that her sole mission in life was to save the planet from the materialistic ways of the world. Well, the younger one loved the materialistic lifestyle, dressed accordingly and did not feel the earth needed to be saved. It was obvious that some of the wife's genes had been transferred to her!

Anyway, one day my hippy daughter after having spent several years in USA chaining herself to trees to ensure that the logging industry did not cut them down, decided that she needed to tour India and endeavour to try and save the planet from this location. So she landed up in Mumbai and within a few days hopped into an unreserved coach in the train to Kanyakumari as she felt that this was where her Indian journey should begin. Incidentally, her parents also happened to have a friend in Kanyakumari who was willing to put her up. I am sure this played a major role in influencing her decision. She had no idea as to what she wanted to achieve but decided to go with the flow. She was sure we old-timers were way past our expiry date so any advice from us was only worthy of going in from one ear and exiting from the other.

After spending a few fruitless days in Kanyakumari, she decided that she had worked enough and needed a holiday and so off she was to the beaches of Kerala. I can't imagine anyone of my generation being so casual about not having a job and being pig-headed enough to make sure a holiday is not forfeited at any cost. This just proved the old adage - parents earn, travel economy to save every penny for their children to splurge and travel business class. At this point I decided come what may, I will splurge on a second home when the time is ripe and not leave all my money for my hippy daughter to go save the earth.

A few days later, we got a late night call from our dear daughter to tell us that she had met the man of her dreams on the beaches of Kerala and that he happened to have come there from Brazil on a similar earth saving mission. Well, what can one say? The Kerala beach had brought the Indo-Brazil pair together and soon they were married.

A year later they moved to Berlin and one day my daughter called up with the good news that she was pregnant and had decided to name the baby RAVEN since she saw a lot of ravens in the sky while cycling to her gynecologist's office. Of course, the wife had

a panic attack as this is a name unheard of in India except while referring to a crow, but she gradually settled down when one of her friends told her that it is quite common for a girl in the West to be called Raven.

So now that we had decided to build a house in the Nilgiri Mountains, peace had returned to our house and the next task was to find an appropriate name for this mountain retreat. Since you are aware of my personality, you can be sure I was blank when names had to be suggested. My vocabulary consisted only of medical names and I was sure nobody in their right mind would name a house after a muscle or body part, so I held my silence. The wife, on the other hand, had a new list every day and it was my duty to nod politely and say all were great names and that I felt confident that she would make the right choice. Obviously this pleased her to no end and the lists kept getting longer and I followed my policy of least resistance, although we were not getting any nearer to finding a suitable name. I felt this whole exercise was being blown out of proportion. After all what is so great about choosing a stupid name?

Finally, the wife took off to attend a wedding in Canada and I could have my breakfast in peace without having to go through the daily ritual of meticulously scrutinizing a whole bunch of names and giving my not-so-expert comments which were trashed anyway.

Early one morning, I received a very excited call from Canada. "Hi, have I woken you up? Were you asleep?" I thought, "Well I sure as hell was asleep - but not anymore, thanks to your stupid phone call." But being a good Indian husband, I categorically denied that her phone call had anything to do with my being awake at this unearthly hour of 4 am. Her excitement stemmed from the fact that she had at last hit upon an ideal name. "While driving through the Rockies, I realized that the Raven is worshipped by the Native American Indians here and it is the official bird of many of these tribes. So I have decided to name our mountain retreat RAVEN's NEST after our little grand–daughter!"

I jumped out of bed. It was a 'wow' moment. The wife had outdone herself and hit a jackpot as far as I was concerned. This was a very apt name for a retreat in the mountains and I was sure my hippy daughter and our little grand-daughter would be thrilled with this choice. So this answers the question of **'why'** the name or what's in a name!

CHAPTER 3

HOMESTAY CONCEPT

AND NOW WE come to the **third 'why**'- why a homestay? Generally, anyone building a house in the mountains would want some privacy and relaxation - far from the madding crowd. But now that you are well-acquainted with the lady of the house, can you imagine her sitting all alone amongst the tea bushes and doing nothing? That is definitely a no. No - she needs company! And how does one get company in the wilderness - open a homestay.

Having said that, how does one open a homestay in the Nilgiris? Easier said than done; this we found out much later.

The government of India wants to encourage tourism, they want foreign tourists to get a personal feel of the real India and they hope to achieve this by encouraging homestays. The wife had stayed in a charming one when she attended the high flying Jaipur Literature Festival and had also heard about the popular ones in Coorg. So she was gung-ho on opening one in the Nilgiris as she had been told that the Indian

government was helping in a great way to get you started. Little did she know that the rules in each state are different and opening a homestay in the Nilgiris is a totally different ball game. She realised this much later down the road.

So thanks to the wife's insistence on having company in the hills, a homestay was planned. Fortunately, a wise friend of ours said that when you plan the house make sure there are two independent sections, one for your private residence and one for the guests in the homestay. That was a very sage advice and thus our plans to open a homestay in the mountains called Raven's Nest were finally conceived!

Part 2

Pregnancy

From conception to *birth usually takes nine months but in this case, building Raven's Nest took nine years!*

Chapter 4

Finding Land

Well our first goal was to get a piece of land in the Nilgiris and then build our dream house. Before venturing down this path, we consulted some friends who were the so-called experts in buying land. Our friend in Kanyakumari, in whose house our hippy daughter spent a few days before embarking on her holiday to Kerala which ultimately led to the birth of Raven, said that land was cheap in the Nilgiris, especially in Kotagiri where one of his distant cousins owned a tea factory.

The Nilgiris have a few well-known towns like Ooty, Coonoor, Wellington, and Kotagiri. We decided to explore Ooty first as it is known as the 'Queen of Hill Stations'. But one look at Ooty put us off completely as there was so much of unregulated construction work, no greenery and chaotic traffic. It may have been worthy of the title during the British Raj but in its present condition it is a shadow of its past glory.

Coonoor seemed slightly better with some stately houses and lush green tea estates. Unfortunately, the latter were being gradually sub-divided into small segments to be parceled off for house plots in the near future. Thus, Coonoor was soon, very likely, to lose its pristine charm and follow in Ooty's footsteps. Coonoor, however, had a very robust social life and this would have suited the social cravings of my dear wife, but what prevented us from looking any further in Coonoor was the land prices which were atrociously high, even more expensive than some of the suburbs of Mumbai.

Wellington hosts the Armed Forces Staff College, the Wellington Club and a lovely golf course. Most of the land here belongs to the Army and the rest has already been sold to golf addicts who want to live a stone's throw (in this case a golf ball's throw) away from the club.

So by default, it had to be Kotagiri, which was considered downmarket at that time and not well known to the Mumbai crowd. Fortunately, the wife had an uncle in Coonoor who was a very generous host and knew everyone in town. He arranged a meeting with our Kanyakumari friend's cousin, the Kotagiri Tea Factory owner. However, when we told him our budget and requirements, he just laughed and told us to go back to Mumbai as he was certain that we would not get anything for that price.

A few days after our return to Mumbai, we got a frantic call from the Tea Factory owner and he told us to come back immediately as he had located some land at the price we wanted. Now that we had just returned to Mumbai and the wife was busy with her party circuit, there was no way she was going to take a flight back to survey the property, so she did the next best thing and requested her Coonoor uncle to visit the property and give his feedback. The feedback she got a few days later was depressing as he said that there was no view from the property. So we did not bother anymore.

Three days later another frantic call was made by our Kotagiri friend asking us about our decision regarding the property. When the wife told him that her uncle thought it was not worth it, she got a mouthful! "Are you buying the property or is your uncle? You better come down here immediately, see the property and then take a decision." The wife quietly took the next flight down south and my admiration for the Tea Factory friend went up several notches as he was able to successfully bully the wife into thinking along his lines - something I dare not even think of doing!

The first sentence the wife heard on meeting our Kotagiri Tea Factory friend was "This property has a well on it and any time you buy a property in the hills you have to worry about the long term water supply. Here you are getting it gift-wrapped so don't hesitate to buy it. Even if you don't like it, you can sell it in future." This conversation was relayed to me verbatim and I told her to please go ahead and buy it as this was the first time in our lives that we had some money and the price was within our budget. Our predicament reminded me of the popular US television show 'The Price is Right'.

Thus, the first part of the land was bought site unseen. The plot in the valley was easily accessible by a tar road, thanks to its proximity to that of a powerful politician neighbour's. Unlike the views in other hill stations, this one didn't command that of the plains below, but of the majestic blue mountains around. Then, our land did not have the tall silver oaks that shimmered in the sun like those in our neighbour's land. The previous owner had shorn the land off the trees and sold it for a hefty price to a plywood factory in Mumbai. The missing view and trees didn't bother us, but we soon discovered that they bothered the tea, some of which was rust-coloured unlike our neighbour's rich green tea bushes.

We discovered that the tall mountains had generous gaps between them that allowed the cold, moist air to descend into the valley as frost and settle on the bushes, which without the tree cover, turned our leaves to the colour of a coffee decoction instead of the fresh green hue.

Normally, in a hill station, the beauty lies in looking down from the top of the mountains into the fertile valley. However, here we had to change our orientation and start looking up from the valley of half dead tea bushes and view the greenish, thickly forested, majestic mountain peaks in the distance. No wonder the wife's uncle had mistakenly rejected the property for having no view.

CHAPTER 5

EXPERT LAWYER

HAVING IDENTIFIED THE property, next came the actual buying and since we were not locals, we felt it was essential to hire a good lawyer to scrutinise all the documents. The wife told the lawyer that we wanted all the documents to be in order with the T's crossed and all the I's dotted since we were from Mumbai and that was how it was done there. Our extremely professional lawyer very calmly said, "Don't worry ma'am, there are over 18 cousins who own this property and I will study all the papers meticulously and get all their signatures along with those of their heirs so you won't have any problem in the future."

Hearing him say this, I realised that all the legal loopholes would be plugged and there would be very little chance of our property going the RRR way.

In Mumbai, the news headlines on all the TV channels and newspapers was about the plight of the Raiz Rayne Residency Complex (RRR) residents, many of whom had bought their flats in the mid 1980's with their hard-earned money and were now facing

demolition threats due to some unscrupulous builders who had bought the adjoining plots of land and wanted to usurp the prime RRR property. The RRR Complex residents who were in a no-win situation, were finally able to get some breathing space, thanks to the superb media coverage which brought the facts to the fore, ultimately resulting in most political parties supporting and helping them.

Land transactions in the hills are notoriously cash transactions and we had a tough time convincing all the sellers that if they got full cheque payments from us, they would not get into any trouble. Fortunately all agreed and we were able to buy the property in a complete 'white' transaction which was unheard of then. The revenue department must have been happy as they got a substantial amount in stamp duty.

Once the deal was registered, we proudly drove up to the land and, as was the custom, were presented with a few tea leaves from the garden to seal the deal. The wife then said, "Let's fence the land as initially we will be absentee landlords and we don't want any squatters." Our lawyer very sheepishly said, "Madam, please look around - do you see any other land fenced?"

He was right. There were no fences. Each property was demarcated with a few white stones that were difficult to locate and nobody ever thought of encroaching on another's property. This made for a very harmonious, neighbourly co-existence.

Chapter 6

Shortlisting Architects

Now that we had bought our property, we needed a good architect and a contractor to build our dream house. Without batting an eyelid the wife immediately shortlisted five hotshot architects from Mumbai whom she or her friends knew from the cocktail circuit. I had been told that it was always better to use a local architect as they would be familiar with the weather pattern in the Nilgiris and the material best-suited for house building in those conditions. But dare I venture a suggestion at this juncture seeing that the wife was in overdrive?

But miracles do happen. Some of the Mumbai architects were too busy and others had no idea where Kotagiri was and were thus not inclined to have their name associated with a downmarket place.

Kotagiri is very accessible from Mumbai. There are five daily direct flights from Mumbai to Coimbatore International Airport which also boasts of direct connections to Singapore and Sharjah. Long distance taxis are freely available here, and the picturesque

drive from the airport to DOWNTOWN Kotagiri takes only two hours. The road is in excellent condition as the most famous Lady of Tamilnadu has an estate in Kotagiri. She, of course, has a private helipad and reaches there by helicopter but her flunkies who love to prostrate in front of her, drive up whenever she is there, so the road has to be in top condition. It really is a very pleasant drive and in fact, travel is so hassle-free that one can have breakfast in Mumbai and lunch in Kotagiri.

I was glad that the Mumbai architects were not aware of the accessibility or the political significance of Kotagiri, for I am sure they would have made a beeline for this place. The other problem the Mumbai architects would have faced was getting the roof right. As we observed many houses in the surrounding areas, we realised that those built by the local architects had nice high-tiled slanting roofs whereas those built by the 'PLAINS' architects had flat cement roofs which invariably leaked after the second monsoon. 'PLAINS' is a term used contemptuously for anyone who is not from the hills and this is even more evident when a driver spits the word out.

Driving in the hills needs experience and one has to follow the rules diligently especially when it comes to allowing traffic coming uphill the right of way and being cautious when overtaking. Drivers who are accustomed to driving in the hills follow these rules, but whenever there is a rash overtaking or a car trying to speed dangerously around a curve, you can be sure it is a 'PLAINS' driver.

Road discipline is so good that even the buses give right of way to small cars moving uphill. This would never happen around Mumbai where Might is Right, the bigger the vehicle, the greater the road power. In fact, my driver from Mumbai would have a tough time driving here as his aim is to get from point A to point C in the shortest possible way, even if it means bypassing point B. Thus weaving in and out of traffic, cutting lanes, overtaking from the wrong side of the road, veering between the gaps is in his DNA(Deoxyribonucleic acid). He will never be able to adhere to the hill traffic discipline and will surely find himself tumbling down the hill, taking a scenic view from Kotagiri to the 'PLAINS'.

But all is not gold. The hill drivers have their own set of problems - there are no traffic signals in Kotagiri save for one blinking amber light. So when my hill driver first took the Madam to Coimbatore for shopping, she got the shock of her life (fortunately no heart attack), since our champion F1 driver had no clue that he had to stop at the red light and when she shouted a warning to him, he happily stopped in the middle of the traffic junction. Maybe, there they refer to these characters as 'HILL' drivers.

CHAPTER 7
PERMISSION HEADACHE

We located an excellent architect who had the time and patience to listen to all our requirements, put them together and conceptualise a lovely house plan. Of course, this plan was changed several times before we thought it was right. However, looking at a drawing never gives you a proper feel of how large the house will be or how small the rooms will be unless one has worked in this field earlier. Having vetted the plans, one was still in doubt whether all was not right and this came to bite us later.

Getting approvals from the panchayat to build a house can take a month of Sundays, so rather than getting frustrated, we just took it in our stride. We decided that while waiting to get the permission to build, we should spend the time fruitfully by planting some tree saplings so that as our house came up, the tree cover would also grow in tandem. We visited the surrounding nurseries and picked up some red spathodea, silver grevillea and white alder cuttings and planted them painstakingly in different corners of the land. We hoped that in the not-so-distant future we would have a beautiful kaleidoscope of colours with a lush deep green tea garden interspersed with large red spathodea and silver oak shade trees and the white alder plants lining the boundary. We also managed to get a few jacaranda cuttings and could not wait for the rich purple flowers to bloom although we were warned that it would take several years.

On one of our visits to the property, our friendly neighbour inquired why we hadn't built anything on the land even one year after buying the property. When we told him that we had applied for the required permissions and were awaiting them before we could start building, he was absolutely shocked. His classic gem of a response was, "What on your own land you have to get permission to build your own house?"

He obviously had no clue that permissions are required and when he mentioned this to his neighbours who had gathered around us to chat; they too were surprised about these permissions. I told him that it was fortunate that he did not have to deal with the BMC (Bombay Municipal Corporation) in Mumbai where even getting a death certificate is an intimidating proposition. But his practical answer to that was, "Why do I need a death certificate - after all I will be dead!"

CHAPTER 8

VAASTU INTRICACIES

FINALLY PERMISSIONS WERE acquired and construction was started. After having lived in a readymade flat all these years, when it came down to constructing a house neither I nor the wife had any clue about how it was to be done. We learnt new words connected with house construction every day: foundation, layout, plinth, shell, etc. were added to our vocabulary.

Our architect was an expert in placing the house. After studying the lay of the land, he chose the perfect spot which also happened to be the highest point, right in the middle of the property, to place the house. He was very familiar with the path of the sun, the flow of the monsoon water and which direction a house in the hills should face. By choosing this high spot he was able to ensure that we would get a panoramic view of the tea garden with its plethora of newly-planted saplings, which one day, would blossom into colourful trees and concurrently, we could soak in the high mountain ranges that formed a very picturesque backdrop in the distance. Thus, our concern of building a house in a valley which had 'no view' was overcome. This reiterated the importance of getting a local architect and I was secretly thankful to the PLAINS architects for turning down the job.

After the land had been leveled, the markings were made on the ground demarcating each room and the boundary walls. Looking at it at first glance, the bedrooms appeared very small, but we were reassured by the contractor that once the foundation was laid and the plinth in place, the rooms would look bigger as they were all built to *Vaastu* measurements. Now, I was no believer in *Vaastu* but obviously everyone around us wanted the house to be *Vaastu*- compliant. When the final product was ready, I felt we had been shortchanged in the size of the bedrooms and we should have insisted on bigger bedrooms even if the measurements did not match the *Vaastu* arithmetic. Like a tube light, I realised that what appeared odd in the initial drawings – the miniscule bedrooms, were a reality I had to accept for it was too late now.

When I mentioned this to an architect friend of mine from Mumbai who visited us several years later, he said, "Don't worry, better to keep the bedrooms small, because you want your guests to spend more time outside enjoying the natural beauty rather than sitting in a large bedroom". That eased my sense of having been shortchanged to some extent and I felt that maybe *Vaastu* did have some merit!

Chapter 9

Foundation Lessons

After the markings had been made, the digging started. On quizzing the contractor as to what the next step was, the surprised look on his face could not mask what was going on in his mind, "These stupid city folks seem to have no clue about house building." That's right, it looked like we had come from a different planet!

He very patiently told us that they were digging the ground to a certain depth and then they would lay the foundation. Since this was a single storey house they didn't have to dig too deep but if it had been a multi-storeyed house they would have had to go deeper. All depended on the height of the house.

This was an interesting conversation which came back to bother me a few years later when the RRR case was going on.

As I had mentioned some time earlier, the Raiz Rayne Residency Complex (RRR) case was making headlines in Mumbai. Basically the builders had been given permission to build eight buildings of five floors each, but they built only six buildings utilising some

of the extra floor space index to build taller buildings. These buildings were constructed in the late 1980's and the residents who had occupied them were facing eviction in the 2010's!

But the query that nagged me was that if permission was granted to build a five-storeyed building, how had they built an eighteen-storeyed building - isn't the foundation different for both? This practical knowledge had been garnered from our Kotagiri contractor who thought we were from a different planet.

So to any sane thinking person it was apparent that the builders and authorities were well aware that an eighteen-storeyed building was coming up on the plot since the depth and strength of the foundation is proportionate to the height of the building. Thus, even before the building construction had started all those conniving crooks had taken a slice of the pie and twenty five years later the innocent building residents were being hounded as the guilty party and the crooks were all scot-free. It appeared to be a travesty of justice.

Once the foundation came up, the contractor said it was better to let it just sit for some time. This would give the authorities time to come and inspect it and check whether it was compliant with the approved plans.

Obviously this step was given a slip in the RRR case!

He also said that if the foundation faces a monsoon, it would set well and the foundation would be solid. I can assure you our foundation faced several monsoons and thus must be extra solid!

Chapter 10

Curing Process

On several consecutive visits, we found that there was very little progress after the foundation stage and the plinth was coming up at a snail's pace. When we questioned this lack of progress, the standard reply was that the longer the shell is exposed to the elements, the better it will cure.

It was only later that we realised who needed curing. The labourers got paid on Saturday and their first stop was the local booze shop which was located 500 yards from our front gate. I can assure you this was not one of the USPs (unique selling points) which convinced us to buy the place.

While driving on the Interstates in USA, signs like "Next Gas stop only 10 miles away - open 24 hours" appear regularly. For the labourers on our house site, they could very well have put up a sign "Liquor shop 500 yards away - open (Saturdays) 24-7!"

The liquor shop was basically a hole in the wall where bottles were stacked from floor to ceiling in a dingy, poorly-lit room with a single dim bulb dangling from a makeshift rafter and a fat, tobacco-chewing person sitting on an uncomfortable chair listening to loud Tamil music. There was no creaking fan as depicted in most western movies since the weather here was cold all through the year. The labourer had to stretch his hand through this small hole, with a fist full of cash and the tobacco chewer happily took the cash and shoved a quarter bottle back in the labourer's hand. Brandy seemed to be the favourite drink and these watering holes were also referred to as 'Brandy shops'. Adjacent to the Brandy hole in the wall shop was a tin shed supported by wobbly bamboo pillars stuck in the floor which was uneven and plastered with a mixture of red soil and cow dung. A few rickety wooden benches were strewn around the room and there was one person behind a small counter serving snacks which consisted of extra spicy, chilly-flavoured ground nuts. If one spent a few minutes observing the customers, the sequence was very predictable. First half the bottle of brandy was gulped to quench the thirst, then the ground nuts were munched in extra fast time and to overcome the spicy taste, the rest of the brandy bottle was emptied down the throat and the hand went back in the hole with a fistful of cash for the next bottle. This process continued till the cash ran dry!

Similarly, the pattern of work was: Saturday afternoon get paid; post tea hit the booze shop with a pocket full of cash. Consume as much as possible on Saturday, sleep right through Sunday, wake up with a hangover on Monday - and call in to say you are sick, family member sick or neighbour sick and has to be taken to the hospital. The work week was thus shortened and the curing was prolonged but obviously it was not of the wall!

CHAPTER 11
BUILD & BREAK

ALTHOUGH WE WERE novices in house building, one step in the construction process struck me as odd and a complete waste of money, materials, time, and effort. I suppose being a surgeon; one tends to be more practical and precise so I could not understand why this step in house construction is not modified.

Reminded me of the RRR case where the authorities wanted the buildings demolished - such a waste of money, materials and human suffering whereas some other solution such as modification of the plans, rules and penalties would have been more practical.

Since I can't have a rational discussion at home, without being shouted at and opposed, I appeal to you my dear reader to tell me if my argument makes any sense.

Before starting construction, all the plans are ready and the positions of the bathrooms and bedrooms are clearly marked out. The foundation and plinth are made of solid concrete blocks over a foot thick and they are laid meticulously and given time to cure to become solid.

When the plumber starts work in the bathroom, at a much later stage, he lays the pipes and then scratches his head as the pipes have to find an outlet from the house. So what does he do? Yes, you guessed it...uses a hammer and chisel to break the concrete to make a hole in the same foundation and plinth. He brings the pipes out and then re-cements the same holes that he has made.

Isn't it possible and more practical, to lay an inlet, outlet pipe in every bathroom at the foundation and plinth stage itself rather than make and break?

The process being followed in the above scenario would be similar to that followed by a surgeon who does an operation to remove an organ, but instead of removing it at the time of surgery, stitches up the patient and sometime later makes another incision to remove the organ!!

Seems a bit weird for a novice like me. Maybe the 'PLAINS' architects can answer this!

Chapter 12

Ship Breaking

WE WERE FORTUNATE that the wife had a large circle of friends who insisted on visiting her to see what she was up to in the wilderness. One such friend who came early in the construction stage wanted to know what type of flooring was going to be used. Here we were struggling with foundation, plinth, curing of the walls and there she was discussing the flooring! That is what I had to deal with, basically putting the cart before the horse.

We frankly told her that we had not reached that far with our planning but she insisted that we needed to have a full wooden flooring as that was what was ideal in the hills. She was also adamant that the wood quality also should be top class preferably old Burma teak. On hearing this and seeing the wife nod her head in agreement, I nearly fainted thinking of how expensive this exercise would turn out and now I would have to start looking for a second job, which unfortunately is not possible in India for a doctor.

In the US it is conceivable for doctors to moonlight in the Emergency Rooms over the weekend to earn the

extra bucks, but in India Medicine is supposed to be an altruistic profession and a doctor trying to earn extra money is looked down upon.

Fortunately, this lady friend had a suggestion on where such wood would be available. Since her family had a shipping business in Goa, she said, "Why don't you find some old ship and get the wood from the deck as that will be well-seasoned old Burma teak wood." Easier said than done - where does one find an old ship for sale????

A few weeks later, a new patient of mine happened to mention that he was from Bhavnagar and his business was ship breaking! There is a large ship breaking industry in Alang near Bhavnagar where ships from all around the world are beached to be broken and their different components sold as scrap. The most sought after component is steel and the least is wood! Bingo it looked like we had hit the jackpot both in quality and price!

Not much after, I accompanied by my carpenter and the wife, who now grudgingly acknowledged that the husband, had some use after all, took a trip to Alang. It was fascinating to see the big ships being broken and in different stages of dismemberment. Like I had mentioned earlier, patients in India still treat their doctors as part of their family and my ship breaking patient was no exception. Thanks to him we were able to visit several ships, wood selling yards and our carpenter could choose the best quality, seasoned wood.

We soon discovered the wood chosen had lined the deck of the '1952 Manila Princess' which was a floating casino in the Philippines and we had seen the ship up close and personal the day before, so we were absolutely certain on the authenticity of the Burma teak wood.

We didn't have to bother too much about the price as my patient who was in the business said he would negotiate the best price for us but we did have to bother about the quantity of wood required.

We had prematurely embarked on this wood purchasing journey since our house was still in the half shell stage, so we had no clue as to how much wood to buy. So, sitting in the ship breaking yard in Alang, we called up our contractor in Kotagiri to find out what quantity of wood was required for the flooring of the whole house. This poor contractor was busy with his curing job (both house and labourers!), so he had no clue as to what was needed and he made a frantic call to the architect who gave the floor dimensions in square feet. Now our carpenter sitting with us in Alang knew about wood quantity only in cubic feet (as that is the norm in Mumbai) and the wood depot owner sold the wood only in metric tonnes (as that is the norm in Alang). So this exercise of converting square feet to cubic feet to metric tonnes took us more time than actually selecting the wood!

Chapter 13

Wood Transport

HAVING BOUGHT THE wood, we now needed to get it transported to Kotagiri and the only mode of transport was an independent truck service. We were asked to choose between a ten wheel truck and an eight wheeler. So another call to our contractor who said that it would be very difficult for a ten wheeler to climb up the hills and that we'd better settle on an eight wheeler. However, we soon realised that the amount of wood we had bought would not fit into an eight wheeler and we had no option but to load a ten wheeler.

We then got our first shock when we asked where the wood had to be insured for the journey (after all it was an expensive piece of merchandise). We were told that there was no insurance coverage for this type of transport and all we could do was to leave it to GOD.

The next shock was when we met the driver who was four feet nine inches tall weighing a mere forty kilos and his feet barely reached the foot pedals! When we told him that his final destination would be Kotagiri - he wanted to know whether it was anywhere near Hyderabad as that was the farthest south he had been.

He had no GPS (Global Positioning System), no maps, and no knowledge of any south Indian language but was confident that he would deliver the wood in four days. Again, leave it to GOD!

We crossed our fingers, said all our prayers and left Alang with a sick feeling that we may not see this wood again, fearing that the driver might indulge in a few drinks, lose his way or that the truck might turn turtle and all our wood be spilled along the highway.

We kept our fingers crossed and hoped for the best until we were startled one early morning by a call from the Karnataka forest checkpost where the truck had been impounded as it did not have proper tax permits. Unfortunately, the driver spoke only Gujarati and the checkpost guard only Kannada and they were arguing about his transporting 'firewood' without a valid licence. Fortunately, the wife who was fluent in Kannada ticked off the guard and told him that it was NOT firewood but old Burma teak which was much more valuable and that he could well have confirmed that all the taxes for transportation had been paid if only he had cared to check the receipts.

I think the checkpost guard had never before faced such a firing from a lady (I am quite used to it!) and he decided that it would be wiser to let the lorry through rather than continue arguing about the merits of Burma teak versus firewood. Not to be outdone by a woman, he did, however, collect some minimal '*chai paani*' (tea and water) money from the driver before he sent him on his way.

Surprisingly our five foot nothing driver easily negotiated the mountainous roads and delivered the 'firewood' as promised on day four! One can only say GOD is great.

Chapter 14

Money Flow

Since the wife was giving all her friends a ball by ball description of the progress of her 'iconic' project in the mountains, suggestions were coming in thick and fast on 'where' to procure 'what'. But a valuable piece of friendly advice from an architect friend was, "Do not start any interior work till you have all your finances ready as money will flow out of your hands like water."

The wife had invested the money she had inherited from the sale of her late mother's house in an upcoming apartment complex in Bangalore. This was being constructed by a reputed builder and one had to pay as each slab/floor came up and the full amount was due at the time of possession. This is norm for most under construction buildings right across India. She was assured that the building would be completed in three years and at that time she felt that she would be able to sell the flat and use the money for Raven's Nest.

However, like most builders who love to start numerous projects simultaneously and never deliver on time, this project also faced several delays. On top of that once completed, the builder failed to obtain an Occupation Certificate (OC) resulting in several potential customers backing out of buying the flat.

RRR had by then become a household name all across India and everybody knew that the flat buyers were in big trouble since the builder had not obtained an Occupation Certificate (OC) and the flat owners were thus technically living in an illegal flat. Before the RRR case nobody bothered about such details as can be seen from the fact that there are over 55,000 occupied buildings in Mumbai without Occupation Certificates. Now the first question a buyer asks while inspecting a flat is, "Have you got the occupation certificate?" Looks like some good has come out of the RRR case after all and builders will be more careful in future and not resort to duping the flat buyer.

After applying a lot of pressure and threatening legal action, the builder finally wilted and obtained the Occupation Certificate. The wife had no trouble selling the flat after that and rich with funds she was empowered to get the interior work done. Let the money flow!

Part 3

Medical Termination of Pregnancy

AN UNEXPECTED EMERGENCY *can cause the Medical Termination of a healthy Pregnancy.*

CHAPTER 15

ROLE REVERSAL

NOW THAT THE finances for the interior work had been secured, we looked forward to converting the shell into a real house and started looking for tiles, furniture, bathroom and light fittings.

Wait a minute, wait a minute, and wait a minute! Abort mission, Abort mission, Abort mission!

The wife last night turned on the computer and by chance happened to read what I had written so far and I was unceremoniously woken up, kicked out of bed and angrily shouted at, "What the hell do you think you are doing, writing this crap?"

"I am the journalist who has attended the Jaipur Literature Festivals." *(Of course no mention of why it was important for her to be seen there mixing with the you know who!)*

"I am the one who wanted to buy a house in the mountains." *(Conveniently forgetting she wanted a house in Goa!)*

"I am the one who decided on a Homestay." *(Sure, so you could have company and strut around!)*

"I am the one who named this Raven's Nest." (*That I accept - but do give credit to the hippy daughter for thinking of the name for your little grand-daughter!)*

"I am the one who bought the land." (*But whose hard-earned money did you use?*)

"I am the one who chose the architect." *(Because all your Mumbai ones did not want this down market job!)*

"I am the one who is going to decide on the interiors and fund it with my own mother's money." *(She had a valid point there!)*

So, being the good Indian husband it is my motto, when confronted with the angry lady of the house, to maintain sanity, agree to everything she says, slink into a corner and let her do what she wants. After all whatever she says is correct (and she has my permission to say so--Ha Ha!!)

So my dear friends who have faithfully been with me on this journey so far, I apologise that I have to do a Medical Termination of the Pregnancy and hand over the reins to the angry wife.

PART 4

IN VITRO FERTILISATION

NEWER TECHNIQUES HAVE *replaced age old practices.*

CHAPTER 16

MEDICAL MIRACLES

NOWADAYS, MEDICINE HAS progressed so much, that a woman does not need a man in the true sense to get pregnant. With the technique of In Vitro fertilisation, pregnancy can occur without a 'husband' being in the picture. Similarly, the wife will now take this story forward after having banished the husband to the dog house.

Of course, I will try and sneak back after the baby's birth. But until then bye bye my dear friends and now get a taste of the wife's literary talent!

Chapter 17

Prolonged Wait

Friends, I have been patient for the last several months. However, the wife who threatened to take over the story has been busy swimming, attending lunches and exhibitions. As a surgeon, once I open up a patient, I need to complete the operation quickly, competently and get the patient off the table as fast as possible. However, writers, such as the wife, need time to mull, get into the mood, and find the right frame of mind to sit in front of the computer, hang a 'Do Not Disturb Sign' and then start doodling! So I have decided to continue while I have a chance but move to another territory lest I get yelled at once again for hijacking the narrative.

PART 5

MORNING SICKNESS

PREGNANCY IS KNOWN *to cause morning sickness.*

Chapter 18

House Demolished

Sickness is also caused by injury, stress, anxiety, and depression. Building a house should not result in any sickness; in fact it should be a happy experience.

But the thought of your house being demolished can cause sickness due to stress, anxiety and depression.

Imagine the money down the drain, no roof over your heads and no resources to buy a new house in the present expensive marketplace.

So why are we suddenly talking about a house being demolished?

PART 6
GESTATION

THE WAITING PERIOD, *while something is developing inside.*

CHAPTER 19

LOCATION CHANGE

WHILE WAITING FOR the wife to get into the 'mood', let's move to another location. You may be wondering why I keep mentioning the infamous Raiz Rayne Residency Complex (RRR) in several places.

In Tamil Nadu, where Raven's Nest is located, many alpha males such as politicians, film stars and industrialists have a big house (*pereeya veedu)* and a small house (*chinna veedu)*. The big house is for the big man and his official wife and the small house is for the big man and his unofficial wife, mistress, keep or whatever you want to refer to her as. So in keeping with this tradition, Raven's Nest was our *pereeya veedu* and RRR was our *chinna veedu*. However, let me assure you that there was no alpha male in this setting as by now you are well aware that this was more a henpecked male, so the additional attributes of the *chinna veedu* were unfortunately missing!

Raiz Rayne Residency Complex (RRR) is located in Prabhadevi and comprises of six multi-storey buildings built in the 1980's. Originally, the land was leased to the owners of the popular drink Meta Mate which had become a well-known name once Mate Cola International was thrown out of India in the 'only *desi* is the best' spirit of one political party which also threw IBM out at the same time. There was a large Mate Cola factory and a lovely garden in this area but thanks to industrial disputes, the owners decided to convert part of the land into a residential complex.

Chapter 20

Evicting Squatters

After obtaining some dubious permission, they sold the development rights to three developers to build the complex. One of these developers was a big smuggler and his job was to evict all squatters from the land.

You may recollect, this was one of our apprehensions when we bought Raven's Nest till our lawyer told us to look around and see if any fences existed on other properties. In Mumbai, squatters are experts in occupying empty stretches of land, putting up bamboo poles and blue plastic sheets as coverings and before long, lo and behold a slum has sprung up right before your eyes. Fortunately, this practice has not caught on in the Nilgiris and is very unlikely to do so as these squatters obviously need political, municipal and criminal patronage to carry on such brazen acts and this is not forthcoming in the hills.

Evicting squatters is a herculean task, as these people are well aware, come the next election most political parties will vie with each other to legalise these squatters who by this time have obtained illegal electric and water connections and converted the property into a regular slum with a large vote bank. The next step is to get a cutoff date for slum rehabilitation extended by the political party in power and before long the squatter has a small flat in a newly constructed slum rehabilitation multi-storey building, all for free! He can then happily rent this out and find his next virgin territory to start his new squatting project.

Since one of the developers in this project was a notorious smuggler, he faced no hurdles in evicting these squatters. The story goes that one night he and his henchmen entered the squatters' colony which occupied the area demarcated for the future RRR. He set up a table and chair bang in the middle of the colony and asked his henchmen to roundup all the squatters and bring them for a 'society meeting'. He plunked a large, sharp, evil-looking knife on one end of the table and a big bag with wads of cash at the other end of the table and called the meeting to order. The agenda was very simple - either take the cash and leave this place or face the knife and leave this place. I don't think there was much discussion at the meeting which ended in record time and obviously the sharpness of the knife blade was never tested!

Chapter 21

Black Holes

There are numerous black holes in the universe about which nothing is known and much of what happened in the quarter century between 1980- 2005 would qualify RRR to find a place in one of them. As scientists have recently started unearthing the mysteries of these black holes, the RTI (Right To Information Act) of 2005 played a major role in bringing the misdeeds surrounding RRR to the fore. Much of what actually happened is gleaned from this source.

Although Raven's Nest took a fairly long time to build (a month of Sundays!) mainly due to the extra-long curing process, RRR was completed in a record short time in spite of numerous stop work notices. Police teams were also called in to implement these stop work notices, but if a developer is an expert in getting rid of squatters, he evidently will not have any problem in doing the same with the police.

Thus RRR gathered strength from floor to floor and the flat buyers kept on shelling out their money as and when each floor was completed with the hope that they would become proud owners of the flat once the building was ready.

Fortunately in Raven's Nest, we already owned the land and once the building was constructed we were proud owners of the building and the land.

However in RRR, the flat buyers owned only the flat and not the land on which their building stood, as the clever developers never conveyed the land to them!

This was one of the lessons learnt and the reason for insisting on a very competent, meticulous lawyer who would dot all the I's and cross all the T's while buying the land in the Nilgiris.

Chapter 22

FSI Division

ONCE THE SQUATTERS had been successfully evicted, the three developers had a mini party and decided to divide up the land amongst themselves. How this was done is anybody's guess as they wrapped up the division in the realms of legal jargon that even a modern day Einstein would not be able to fathom.

Even the eighteen cousins who had subdivided the ownership of the Raven's Nest property were no match for this gang of three when it came to carving out small niches of land. Maybe Mao's Gang of Four would have been a better match for them.

This intricate subdivision of land has resulted in numerous fights even at the present time, with each building in RRR claiming larger swathes of land in order to garner more floor space index (FSI). FSI is dearer than gold in Mumbai as this is the amount of space a builder gets to put up a building and it is directly proportional to the land area he has been allocated.

Once each of the three had determined how much land was theirs, they calculated the FSI each was entitled to and went about their merry way and started constructing their coveted buildings little realising or bothering about the fact that the other guy was consuming more FSI than he had been allotted.

The initially approved plan was for constructing eight buildings of five floors each, but in keeping with their mindset that approved plans are only for the dustbin, the gang of three built six buildings, each with more than five floors, stating to the whole world that their individual building was as per approved plans/FSI.

In Raven's Nest, our architect was very particular that all plans get approved and the FSI used was as per plan with the building being laid out in the correct place for he wanted to ensure that nobody would have to face any problem in the future.

However in RRR, the developers were least concerned about this aspect as their main goal was to put up a building, sell the flats, collect the money and run. Unfortunately all of them have run through the black hole to the other world by now.

Since we had already learnt a lesson on the relation between foundation and height of a building from our hills contractor, it was obvious to us that this gang of three 'PLAINS' architects were not bothered about doing anything the legal way but depended more on their sharp knife or bag of cash.

The whole RRR Complex had been constructed in a blatantly dishonest manner and it was apparent that the authorities of that period who were assigned the task of inspecting the building from the foundation stage just dug into the bag of cash, turned a blind eye and never imagined that a quarter of a century later the

RTI Act would bring light into the black hole and all their misdeeds would be exposed.

The first building was completed in the mid 1980's and the buyers who had been pouring in their hard-earned money floor by floor were eager to move into their new homes. Before starting to move in, they casually asked about the Occupation Certificate which the developer assured them to be obtained in the next year or two when all the other buildings were completed and the whole complex was ready. This seemed a genuine reason for not having obtained an Occupation Certificate and these poor owners who had stretched themselves with their life savings invested in these flats and with nowhere else to stay, decided to move in and wait for the rest of the complex to be completed.

Little did they realise that moving in without an Occupation Certificate was illegal and that this would come to bite them a quarter century later and earn the whole RRR Complex a national notoriety.

Quite different from what the wife faced while selling her flat in Bangalore as by then RRR was in the limelight and all the potential buyers insisted on an Occupation Certificate. In fact most brokers in Mumbai are crying now as new flat purchases have hit a roadblock with buyers insisting on having all documents upfront unlike in the good old days when a buyer was willing to wait for them after moving in.

CHAPTER 23

OCCUPATION CERTIFICATE

WHAT IS THE biggest problem one faces when moving into a building without an Occupation Certificate (OC)?

No water and higher taxes. One can live with the higher taxes. But can one live without water? I don't think so. The alternative is to hire tankers to get water to the building and that costs a bomb with rates being jacked up pre-monsoons, when the wells run low. Water tankers visiting posh buildings is a common sight in Mumbai and only after we became aware of the problems in RRR did we realise that there are so many other buildings without OCs in Mumbai.

While initially buying the land for Raven's Nest, our tea factory friend had insisted that it was a wise investment as there was a well on the land. He knew the importance of water and all the people in the Nilgiris understand this as agriculture is water-dependent but we, city people, did not quite comprehend why he was so gung ho about a well on the land. As time went by, we did dig another well and went in for rain water

harvesting in Raven's Nest so that we were totally self-sufficient in the water department.

Since the water tanker prices kept on moving northwards, some geniuses in RRR decided that enough was enough and felt they should approach the courts to get water and while they were at it, they opined that it would be wise to ask the courts to direct the Municipal Authorities to legalise the buildings.

The saying 'let sleeping dogs lie' has a lot of merit and little did the geniuses realise that by approaching the courts, they were about to stir up a storm over which they would have no control.

Chapter 24
Water Woes

The court system in India is like a meandering river – keeps on flowing with various twists and turns and no end in sight. So once a case is filed it just drags on with numerous adjournments and new dates for hearings as one of the parties is invariably busy on the appointed court appearance day. This results in the initial enthusiasm evaporating and as the case drags on, the representation from both parties gets thin and finally only the lawyers are there, smacking their lips and ever ready to collect their legal fees; thanks to another technical adjournment of the case.

Similarly, the RRR water case dragged on and on till a new judge came on the bench and decided that it was high time he got rid of all the backlog of cases. He strictly instructed the lawyers to have all their clients present at the next hearing as he wanted to dispose off the case. However, lawyers being lawyers they took it in their stride, misread the judge's intention and did not bother to inform the municipal authorities that their presence was also required at the next hearing.

The judge walked in to the court on the said hearing day, saw the two lawyers there, one representative from the RRR genius group, who happened to be in the vicinity and had dropped in by chance to see what the inside of a court room looked like and no municipal representative present. He was furious as this was a direct challenge to his authority and shouted at the lawyer representing the Municipal Authority that he wanted the Secretary there in thirty minutes or else he would send him to jail for contempt of court!

Lo and behold, it appeared like a terrorist bomb had detonated. There was lot of running around, SOS sent to all municipal departments and within twenty eight minutes a harried Assistant Secretary who had just returned to office after a two month holiday was rushed to the court and made to stand before a fuming judge. Poor chap faced a severe dressing down from the judge for his earlier non-appearance and to compound it as he had not heard about this case before; he had no answers to any of the judge's questions.

The judge kept repeating, "Why does this RRR Complex have no water even twenty years after construction?"

Unfortunately, this official was in no way connected with the ward in which RRR was located, and hence was clueless about what RRR meant and what the case was all about. He just happened to be in the wrong place at the wrong time and must have been wishing that he had somehow extended his holiday.

Or visited the nearby liquor (Brandy) shop and called in sick like our Monday morning Nilgiri construction workers! He should have taken a lesson from these fellows.

CHAPTER 25

ENRAGED JUDGE

THE JUDGE WAS shouting and the Assistant Secretary (AS) was shivering.

Although I was not privy to this famous court hearing, I garnered from hearsay that it was very entertaining and went something like this:

Judge: "What is the problem with RRR?"
(AS): "Sir, what is RRR?"
Judge: "You idiot don't you know what RRR is? Someone please educate him."

A few minutes after the education lesson,

(AS): "Sir, RRR has no OC, sir."
Judge: "Why no OC?"
(AS): "I don't know sir."
Judge: "Find out you idiot. Someone please educate him."

After several frustrating minutes,

Judge: "I can't be wasting more time. Why no water for RRR?"

Before his lawyer could instruct him,

(AS): "No rains, lakes are dry sir!"

Judge: "You idiot. RRR has no municipal water connection. No OC although it was built twenty years ago. Without an OC you do not get a municipal water connection. So lakes being dry has no bearing on this case. Water is a fundamental right of every citizen. Go do something about this in the next forty-eight hours."

The Assistant Secretary, sweating profusely, left the court in a hurry and scrambled back to the safety of his office and immediately reported the court proceedings to his seniors obviously failing to mention that he was often referred to as an 'idiot'. Maybe if he had, a case could have been registered against the Judge, leading to some entertainment as there would have been a media frenzy while the case got dragged through various courts.

But with the forty-eight hour notice dangling above their heads like the swords of Damocles, the AS had no other thought in his mind except to find a suitable solution.

CHAPTER 26

GENIUS SOLUTION

THE WISE JUDGE had asked the AS to find a solution hinting that water is a fundamental right thus trying to guide him down the correct path. But this subtle suggestion which would have led to a solution did not register in the 'idiot' AS's head.

He went by the book and his thought process went something like this:

'This RRR has no OC.'
'No OC means no water.'

'How do I correct the OC problem, since the Judge has asked me to find a solution?'

'Obviously I cannot penalise the officials who had supervised the building construction since they are my brethren and they let this situation come to pass.'

Brings us back to the Raven's Nest foundation, height of the building and plinth being as per approved plans and our architect ensuring that it matched all the plans but inserting his love for Vaastu in the equation.

'So what can I do? Let's make the RRR Complex match the approved plans.'

'And how do I do that? Simple – demolish all the floors that are not in the initial plans.'

Eureka, a solution had been found and our 'idiot' AS was sure that the Judge would now refer to him as a 'genius'.

Chapter 27

Harsh Judgment

SO SOMETHING AKIN to a double whammy happened there.

Thanks to the geniuses in RRR who raked up this case and thanks to the AS's stroke of genius, an order was passed.

DEMOLISH ALL THAT IS NOT AS PER APPROVED PLAN.

As you may recollect, the approved plan was for eight buildings of five floors each, but only six buildings were built and the unused available FSI was used for building more floors.

But this aspect was completely ignored in the order and it translated to "demolish anything above the fifth floor".

This literally meant that in an eighteen storey building you needed to demolish thirteen floors and leave the lower five standing without causing any damage to the structure of the building. I am sure even the most renowned 'PLAINS' architect would have had a tough time carrying out this project.

Chapter 28

Obtain Stay

Word spread like wild fire in RRR that a demolition order had been passed. Of course, the culprit genius gang that was responsible for igniting the fire had conveniently disappeared. A few volunteers were left with the unenviable task of dousing the fire in the shortest possible time as the AS had made this order applicable within five days. How he arrived at a five-day notice period is anybody's guess, but presumably he felt it would synchronise well with his above five-floor demolition order.

RRR volunteer team was clueless as to what they should do next. None of them were lawyers and they spent two precious days running around like chickens without heads. They had no funds to consult a lawyer and so depended on a cousin of a cousin to get some free legal opinion.

A lawyer who is not paid is not going to give you the best advice or bother too much about the case. His one line answer was, "Get a Stay."

Now to get a stay, you need a lawyer and to get a lawyer you've got to pay. To pay you need money and RRR which had no water had no money! So a collection hat was passed around all the buildings and some funds were raised. The first red flag at this stage was that about a dozen members vehemently refused to pay stating that their flats were legal. In the hurry of getting something concrete done, this red flag was ignored and it came to bite us later.

There are big name lawyers in the Supreme Court who fly around in jets or fool around in their offices with their lady brethren and charge a bomb. Fortunately, we were not in the big courts but in the small teeny weenie lower court where the lawyers charge less but with our cash crunch, we had to look for the bargain basement sale.

We finally zeroed in on a lawyer who had been dubbed 'The King of Stays' and his mannerism and dress was very similar to another King – Elvis, 'The King of Rock'. After much bargaining (yes, you can bargain with lawyers - but the legal term used is negotiation), out of the goodness of his heart, he agreed on a rock bottom price as a special case. Whether this was true or he had no 'stays' in the pipeline is debatable.

True to his title, he easily got us a stay but little did we realise that the foundation on which he had built his case for the stay was very weak.

In Raven's Nest, we had a solid foundation built by experts which had been cured over several monsoons. The interior work started only when the money was ready as a friend had warned the wife that money will flow like water while the interior is being done.

On the other hand in RRR, we had a very weak foundation for the case as we had hired the shadiest 'King of Stays' lawyer who had very little time to prepare a sound case. Our fund situation was very poor as some refused to pay. Both these factors came back to haunt us as the RRR saga unfolded.

Chapter 29

Obituary Columns

Being very familiar with the court system which is akin to a meandering river, the 'King of Stays' kept on getting us one stay after another and all at RRR became complacent. This appeared like a series of olden day cricket test matches which invariably petered out into a boring five-day drawn match, test after test. All one had to do was switch on the transistor radio (later era TV) at the end of the day to know what little had been achieved on the field.

Very little was achieved in the court too, and the only indication that another stay had been granted was a hand-delivered letter with the bill which arrived promptly the next day. No need to listen to the transistor radio or watch the TV in this case.

This pattern continued for several years and nobody paid much attention when the hand-delivered letters stopped arriving, as all were busy with their normal lives and had forgotten that a demolition sword was hanging over RRR.

One day, at breakfast my dear wife raised her head from the newspaper and said, "Oh by the way, do you know your lawyer died a few months ago? It was in the papers and I forgot to tell you." I was sure that this news was authentic as she took pride in reading 'The Times of India' daily mainly to check the obituary page and see who has disappeared in the black hole.

My problem with the obituary page is that I still cannot decide what sort of photograph I should earmark for this page. Obviously not one of those from my Nilgiri school days. Every time I see a youthful photo, I feel sorry that such a young life has been cut short prematurely and then looking at the date of birth, realise that it is a picture of someone who is over ninety years old. I have vowed never to make the same mistake in my case.

But then I won't be there to make this choice. So I need to keep two sets of mature photos, one with a happy face shot in Raven's Nest and the other with a sad face shot in RRR and let the younger generation decide which to publish. After all they need to take some decisions such as who is going to inherit Raven's Nest and who is going to be stuck with the RRR litigation.

Soon after breakfast, I called up the chief volunteer and passed on the bad news. He didn't seem perturbed as he believed that the son who up until now was the 'Prince of Stays' would take over the title of the 'King of Stays' and continue the good work his dad had been doing. By now he certainly would have mastered the technique and we should have nothing to worry about.

Little did he know how wrong he was and that a tsunami was going to hit RRR very soon.

CHAPTER 30

BUILDER CONNED

IN THE NILGIRIS, once the land is bought and registered in your name, it sure as hell belongs to you. So the land surrounding Raven's Nest cottage where the British had planted the famous Nilgiri tea belonged to us. Talking about the British, you can't help but admire their spirit of adventure, when you think back to the old days when the place was all uncharted territory covered by thick jungle, home to several ferocious wild animals. They had taken it upon themselves to explore these hills and carve out a mini Britain there by building beautiful bungalows surrounded by lush tea gardens.

As opposed to this, in RRR there were no lush gardens and the land did not belong to the flat buyer.

As alluded to earlier, part of the Mate Cola factory land was converted into a residential complex in the 1980's and the owners held on to the other industrial part. Cut to the mid 2000's, and the owners needed more cash, so what did they do?

Sell part of the industrial land to a big builder.

They figured if the famous smuggler could get the squatters out in the 1980's, a big builder could ramrod his way through in the 2000's. The builder, obviously, was also of the same opinion as he had mega plans of building a seven star hotel there.

He confidently submitted his seven star hotel development plan to the authorities and must have been devastated when they rejected his plans. He then re-submitted his plans, on the advice of his astrologer, for a five star hotel as he was told that five seemed to be a favorite number with the powers that be. Remember demolition above five floors. Notice period of five days.

But this tactic also did not work. So the astrologer was fired. I wonder whether he had predicted this fate in his own horoscope.

The big builder along with his political cronies, who had parked their ill-gotten wealth with him, marched down to the Muncipality to find out why permission for their five or seven star mega hotel project had been denied. After all, didn't this already crowded city need a few more seven star hotels?

After several fruitless meetings, several more bags of cash exchanged hands; and he was finally let in on the big secret. "You have been conned. No building can come up here as long as the RRR case is in court and their FSI problem is not resolved."

William Congreve in 1697 in his play 'The Mourning Bride' said, "Hell hath no fury like a woman scorned."

In 2007 these lines could just as easily have been changed to, "Hell hath no fury like a builder conned."

The big builder cussed, cursed, popped in several antacids, nearly had a heart attack and swore he would fix someone for this rip off.

The easiest target for him were the naïve RRR residents who were blissfully unaware of the precarious situation they were in as their oxygen supply was in the hands of the 'Prince of Stays' and this was ultimately controlled by the lower courts.

The builder and his cronies prepared well and struck this hapless target powerfully.

When a tsunami hits, the oxygen supply gets cut off.

Chapter 31

Vacate Stay

THE BIG BUILDER had no problem in getting the stay vacated in the lower court. Either the 'Prince of Stays' had not graduated to the 'King of Stays' or bags of cash had played a major role.

RRR was thrown into turmoil again with a five-day demolition notice re-surfacing like a bad penny. The same scenario played out again, chicken without heads kept running around and now the march was to the higher court. The only lesson learnt, because of the previous premature departure of our lawyer, was that instead of hiring one 'king' for the whole complex, it appeared to be a wiser decision to hire seven (magnificent seven), one for each of the six buildings in RRR with one standby.

Most residents were happy with this line of thinking as they felt there would be safety in numbers. The more the legal minds, the merrier the scene.

It was only when the money collection matter came up again, the same dirty dozen held out with the same argument which was sounding more like a stuck long playing record by now. But who cared - the job had to be done.

The case went on smoothly in the High Court over a few months till one day, suddenly out of the blue, it was put up for hearing in a new court. There was a frantic search for the magnificent seven who were busy elsewhere on another case and some on vacation. So at the last minute, a junior lawyer from the firm was located in the canteen and pulled out in front of the irate Judge; very similar to the petrified AS appearing before an impatient Judge. Only the shoe was on the other foot this time and the RRR lawyer was at the receiving end and not the lawyer representing the MunicipalAuthorities.

In the Nilgiris, one of the common animals seen is the bison. It is a majestic huge black animal, akin to an oversized muscular bull, with white bands around the ankles resembling anklets. Although these animals weigh several tons, they are capable of jumping several feet from a standing position. In the Mother Goose poem which mentions "the cow jumped over the moon", I suppose the author mistook the bison for a cow since the cow is incapable of jumping. The bison is a very peaceful animal that does not bother anyone and it used to stroll into Raven's Nest property during the construction stage to have a drink of water from the open pond. The only time a bison gets aggressive is when it has a calf by its side. In such cases about seven bison surround the calf and protect it from all harm as they realise these young creatures are vulnerable.

In the RRR case the magnificent seven lawyers were not there to protect their junior and this vulnerable junior got chewed up by the opposition.

Surprisingly, in spite of the senior lawyers not being present, the case was heard. The junior's pleas for an adjournment fell on deaf ears and by the end of the evening an order was passed upholding the demolition notice.

A lesson in speedy justice had been just dished out.

Chapter 32

Midnight Meeting

Justice was speedy, but the RRR residents were speedier.

Immediately, they decided the best solution was to wave a white flag and enter into a truce agreement with the big builder as they realised fire power aka money power was needed to win this battle and the RRR coffers were empty. The coffers would never fill up especially with the dirty dozen holding out and refusing to pay their dues.

Again, hearsay from a third party that the meeting with the big builder in a swanky five star hotel of his choice lasted the whole of five minutes. Before the RRR residents could even sit down the builder very arrogantly told them:

"I have the money. You have seen how the court system works. Demolish your flats and leave. Let me build my hotel and then I may consider giving you some place to come back to on payment. If you fight me anymore, you will lose more money in legal fees in the higher courts. I will definitely win as I know the system. In the end you will come crawling back to me on all fours begging for mercy!"

The RRR team went waving white flags but all they saw was a big red flag. It was like waving a red flag in front of a bison (bull) and they came storming out of the meeting, terribly upset and ready for war.

A midnight emergency meeting was called by all the RRR societies.

Similar to our smuggler friend holding a midnight society meeting over two decades ago where the single point agenda was you leave either with a knife stuck in you or with cash in your hand.

This meeting also had a single point agenda: What is the next step?

Midnight meetings are always boisterous as half the crowd has had several rounds of drinks at a party and are itching for a fight and the other half has been woken up from their deep slumber and is not in the best of moods.

Once the members had been brought up to speed about the latest developments and the highlights of the evening's meeting explained briefly, there was total pandemonium. Everyone started shouting, cussing, giving their suggestions and the scene resembled an episode from one of the nightly prime time TV talk show debates where one cannot hear or understand what is being said as all the participants talk at the same time and try to out shout the other.

Finally, after much cajoling and reasoning, some semblance of order was brought to the meeting. It was decided that the big builder along with his cahoots in crime, be it the crooked politicians or municipal authorities, cannot hold us to ransom and we needed to fight back as a united RRR front. The only avenue left was the Supreme Court. It was unanimously decided that the battle should be taken to the Supreme Court which is the ultimate authority for justice.

A few other suggestions of going back to the municipal authorities to see if they could sort this matter out quietly were silenced with loud 'boos' especially from the drinking section of the crowd.

The war cry had been sounded. RRR would go to the Supreme Court.

Chapter 33

Movie Buff

Going to Supreme Court is no big joke. It needs a lot of preparation, time devoted to the cause, money and frequent travel to Delhi. Saying, "Let's go to Supreme Court" after several drinks is quite easy. But who was going to bell the cat and take responsibility to follow it up?

The RRR saga was soon to resemble a masala movie and in every movie there is one hero and one villain.

So who was going to be the Hero in this movie and where would we find this Robin Hood?

In physics, it is said that every action has a reaction. Similarly, in every challenging situation a solution presents itself, if you look deep enough for it.

Robin Hood was in our midst. A very unlikely person, who till now was in his own world, with his own circle of close friends, clueless about what goes on in the world outside or in politics as he did not watch TV or read the newspapers.

Robin, our Hero had obviously not met my wife or else she would have drilled into his head the merits of

reading 'The Times of India' daily to see who appeared on the obituary page. This in turn would have got him into the habit of glancing at the other headlines and he would at least know which political party was in power and which politician belonged to which party. Obviously, our hero was not in the high society party circuit or he would have met her by now.

What about the villain?

Unfortunately, there was no villain at this moment, so the masala movie was on hold. It was just Robin and his band of merry men (and women in this politically correct day and age).

This was a big learning experience and our first lesson was that most Supreme Court lawyers are expensive, busy, take on several clients at the same time, some have terrible tempers and one cannot directly approach them but have to go through an advocate on record (AOR).

They want several meetings to vet the drafts which have been written by the AOR and require your presence there to hammer out a few points or kindle their ego. So Robin made several trips to Delhi but unfortunately always bought the cheapest, standby ticket so he was never eligible for a frequent flyer program.

Robin and his council soon realised that money was burning up like jet rocket fuel and they needed to collect money upfront to hire the best legal brains in Delhi as no lawyer there believed in credit.

Similar to big hospitals that want money prior to admission lest the patient dies and the relatives abscond. It appears very mercenary but that is the reality of the day—Money first, talk later.

It is often said that when it comes to money matters, the true colors of an individual become apparent.

Similarly in RRR, the dirty dozen refused to pay using their time-tested argument that if they had handled the case, we would not have found ourselves with our backs to the wall and supposedly their flats were legal even though they happened to be above the proverbial fifth floor!

They had come to this profound conclusion because their late builder/smuggler had assured them that their flats were all kosher and the problem was only related to the other buildings and he obviously had the papers to prove it. But unfortunately, the papers had disappeared with him into the black hole.

Unlike the movie wherein the Dirty Dozen was a group of tough fighting men, the RRR group needed to hide in the shadows of a thug and fire from his shoulders. In the early 1900s there was a famous mafia Don in Chicago named Al Capone who made his fortune during the prohibition era and numerous movies have been made about his exploits. Our Dirty Dozen was fortunate in finding a modern day Al Capone to lead their cause.

By now you may have realised that I am a movie buff. Most of these movies such as Robin Hood, Magnificent Seven, Dirty Dozen, Al Capone were screened in the Nilgiris where the big town of Ooty has one English cinema theatre called Assembly Rooms and it was very popular with the Laurence school kids.

Raven's Nest unfortunately has no access to a cinema theatre as the only Kotagiri theatre has now been turned into a food plaza, aptly named Bison Park. But in this modern era, home theatres are an ideal substitute and one does not miss the big screen. Fortunately Raven's Nest is so equipped.

Finally, we had all the ingredients for a masala movie. The hero in Robin Hood and his merry men/women and the villain in Al Capone followed by his dirty dozen.

Now my friends fix a drink, sit in a comfortable sofa and enjoy the show. Remember that in a home theatre, you can switch it off whenever you want and return later to continue watching (reading)!

Chapter 34

Money Sharks

Once Robin Hood accepted the responsibility, he plunged into it wholeheartedly. He put on blinkers much like those on the horses, got a tunnel vision on the problem, ignored his wife, left his business on autopilot and became a man possessed with saving all flats in RRR.

Al Capone, on the other hand, continued his façade of being very concerned about the problem but made sure not a rupee was extracted from his flock, as after all, their flats were legal!

It had been decided that no stone should be left unturned while fighting the case in the Supreme Court. Top notch lawyers were hired and all their fees paid upfront.

Paying their fees took some doing as the Dirty Dozen had already backed out and their share had to be borne by the others. There were many in RRR who did not have money to pay their own dues let alone those of the Dirty Dozen. But they tightened their belts and paid their dues (and the extra burden) by mortgaging their jewellery. Desperate times call for desperate measures and a person's true character comes to the fore during these times.

In a desperate situation when a ship is caught in rough weather the saying goes, "any port in a storm" and the sharks keep circling the ship in the hope of it sinking.

Similarly, in Delhi there is a frenzy of sharks known as fixers who are always looking for a ship in distress. Their sole aim is to present themselves as the so-called 'port' to help you beat the storm. They are very sweet talkers, name droppers, know some legal jargon and are extremely confident that they are the messiahs who can rescue you.

They find out which case is going to come up in the Supreme Court and then approach the defendant with a sweet deal promising to fix the case for a hefty price. In other words, implying that bribery and corruption is rampant in the Supreme Court.

They seem to work hand and glove with some of the fly-by-night AORs'.

Listening to these sharks is very depressing because the Supreme Court is the last bastion of Justice, one does not expect money to influence cases but after some digging one realises that these fixers are just playing Russian roulette.

There is a fifty percent chance that the case will go in one's favor and a fifty percent chance that it won't. So if one wins, they collect the money saying that they have swung it in your favour and if one loses, they return the money saying that the other party must have paid a bigger sum!

Desperate people will believe these smooth talking fixers but fortunately, our Robin Hood, although not up with the newspapers, was a shrewd, down-to-earth businessman and he was not as gullible as the sharks expected. He realised pretty fast that this was a big con game and avoided them like the plague since he firmly believed that Supreme Court judges were incorruptible.

Another set of con operators are the AORs'. There are very many reputable ones and a few shady ones. The fixer sharks associate with the latter. These AORs' negotiate the fees for the top notch lawyers who they deal with and one has to go through the AOR to reach the lawyer. The fees are paid to the AOR and one is never sure as to how much actually reaches the lawyer who may get a bad name as the client feels his fees are astronomical, but in reality it is the shady AOR who has pocketed most of the money.

This minority bunch of shady AORs reminds one of brokers who sell you land and jack up the price so that their commission gets higher. But at least in a land deal, one knows how much the land costs as the stamp duty is based on the price of the land. When we bought the land in Kotagiri, it was a full cheque deal, so although the stamp duty was higher than that of a partial cash transaction, we knew the exact amount to be paid to the broker.

Chapter 35
TV Debates

We soon realised that all the top notch lawyers in Delhi have the gift of the gab. This attribute enables many of them to be inducted into political parties.

Unfortunately, doctors are not such expert talkers and their main expertise is in listening to people's complaints in order to treat them, so they are not on many political bandwagons.

This gift of the gab also helps Supreme Court lawyers to find a spot on the evening prime time TV debates loudly defending one political party or the other and tearing their rival party colleague to shreds.

However, that does not prevent them from working harmoniously with this same colleague from a rival political party, if they are unknowingly hired by the same client. Since our main Hero was clueless about political affiliations, he hired two senior lawyers from opposite ends of the political aisle. But being thorough professionals, they gave it their all and used all the lung power that they had strengthened in the TV studios to passionately argue and put up a strong case in our favour in the court.

A strong case is built on a strong foundation and both our Supreme Court stalwarts were unanimous on one point that our initial legal foundation was very weak. If only they could agree so easily on other points in the TV debates, there surely would not be any acrimonious debates, and the ratings of the channels would plunge. Thus the legal foundation of the RRR case was no prime time TV material, but RRR did become a hotly-debated prime time TV topic in a future point in time.

This is when we realised that using the 'King of Stays' had been a Himalayan blunder. The case, as it goes to the higher courts, has to be argued on what was presented earlier and if the initial arguments were on a very narrow point, so be it. Nothing new can be introduced and our 'King of Stays' had stuck to the narrowest point as he was sure he would be able to drag this point till kingdom come, but hadn't realised that he would be dragged into the black hole sooner than anticipated!

Rather than depend too much on the prior imperfectly written legal brief, our two lawyers used their debating talents to the hilt and mesmerised the judges with their sharp, well-researched arguments. Their argument appeared very sound as they said that instead of penalising the current residents of the buildings, the courts should look at the root cause and stem the rot there. They argued that the builders and the authorities who oversaw this project were the main culprits and that they should be punished to send a strong signal that such blatant practices will not be tolerated in the future.

We in the audience were delighted with their long drawn out oratory and now I realised why no doctor can hold a light to the stage presence of these Supreme Court lawyers, who with their command of words can walk into any political party.

Were the Judges also impressed? Only time would tell.

CHAPTER 36

NOSTRADAMUS PREDICTION

ONCE THE ENTIRE long drawn out arguments winded down, the judges asked for a few clarifications and then announced that they would go and ponder over the whole case and give their profound judgment after the holidays.

In the USA, while attending the doctor malpractice insurance meeting, we were assured that in case we were unfortunate enough to face a law suit, the company would send in a crack team of mind reading experts who would help in choosing the jury. They would ensure that only favourable jurors were chosen as this was their area of expertise.

Pity we did not have this crack team in the court room to give us some inkling on what was going on in the judge's mind. Our naïve assessment, not having attended any court previously, was that the judges were swayed by our legal team's Oscar winning performance. Obviously, there is a difference between a biased observation and an objective one. But since there was nobody to contradict us, we stuck to our opinion. We argued that since the judge kept a benign smile on his face all the time, he was in sync with our lawyer's point of view and all was well. So we could go and enjoy the holidays.

The wife, however, was far from convinced about our new found face reading talents and she had dreams of a big wrecking ball hanging over our building and coming down heavily as the chain snaps. I listened to her patiently but knew her dreams were not in the same league as the Nostradamus' predictions but obviously influenced by something nearer home.

I had a large collection of movies and very likely some of my disaster movies were influencing her. It appears that my home theatre in Raven's Nest was being put to good use while I was busy watching the live performance in the courts of Delhi.

The holidays passed uneventfully. Life in RRR continued in the same routine manner till the Judgment day drew nearer. A nervous tension slowly started building up, but people were not too concerned as the biased feedback of the courtroom drama had made the rounds in RRR and it was taken for granted that the judges will return from their well-deserved holiday, having had time to contemplate on the court room performances and put this matter to rest once and for all.

CHAPTER 37

DEMOLISH DEMOLISH

JUDGMENT DAY ARRIVED and unlike in the movies where there is a horde of reporters outside the courtroom shoving a mike into your face and not giving you room to walk, there was hardly any press corps present. I suppose the O J Simpson trial has influenced our perception of how a court trial is conducted.

Besides our lawyers and one RRR resident who happened to be in Delhi for some business and was tasked with being present in the court, the unexpected presence of the previously conned seven/five star hotel big builder with a smirk on his face along with his confident highflying lawyer should have raised some red flags. But now it was too late and all depended on the final judgment.

The benign smiling judge, more appropriately later labeled as the smiling assassin brought out this fifty page document and started reading in a low soft voice, quite unlike the loud authoritative voices of our lawyers. Obviously the judge is not allowed to attend a TV debate and thus has not learnt the art of TV shout talk where the louder one shouts/interrupts others, the more brownie points one scores and more chances of being called back for the next TV debate.

The first forty pages went according to script wherein the judge indirectly agreed with facts set forth by our lawyers during their marathon oration. He, basically, said that all illegal construction occurs under the watchful eye of the town authorities as there is a nexus between the builders and these authorities. This results in a severe strain on the common resources of the city and something drastic needs to be done to control this. He kept quoting case after case and it was apparent that if the lawyers had a gift of the gab, then the judges had a gift of the pen.

Noting the tone of this portion of the recitation, our lawyers and the RRR representative were not only feeling on top of the world but were getting ready to congratulate one another but a red flag continued to flutter as the smirk on the big builder's face had still not been erased.

In cricket, the match is not over till the last ball is bowled. Similarly, till the last page is read, a final decision cannot be made on what the judgment implies. In the last five pages, a googly was bowled, there was a sudden change in the tenor of the text and the rule of five came back to bite us again.

The decision to demolish everything above five floors was upheld. This had to be done in five months. Residents were ordered to vacate the flats in five months. The government had to appoint a five member team to oversee this and none of the government agencies were allowed to lend a helping hand.

The five star hotel builder smirked some more and gave us the 'I told you so look' and we felt that we had been buried under a five foot avalanche with no escape route.

Chapter 38

Pray & Pack

Several legal luminaries who later read the profound judgment in minute detail were stunned at the way the last five pages were completely out of sync with the previous forty page preamble. But judges are always right and a judgment cannot be questioned, you've got to live with it even if you think it is unfair and suspect there is more than meets the eye in the sudden twist in the tale. So RRR had been hung out to dry. Nobody was willing to help us because of the harsh wording of the order and we had no option left.

That is a very frightening situation as your home is going to be demolished for no fault of yours; except for buying a flat without an OC and the main culprits who are the builders and authorities are let off scot free and laughing all the way to the bank.

When all is lost what do you do? Like the movie 'Eat, Pray, Love', RRR got into the pray mode.

Different holy men were called into the compound to lead the prayers. Every religion got a chance – truly secular society. Different teams were formed for weekly visits to temples, churches and mosques. Even a group of eunuchs was asked to do their bit.

In the meantime, some practical residents called in the packers to move their stuff to a godown or a relative's house. The logic was that if your house is going to be demolished, may as well save the contents.

The packers were very professional and had thorough knowledge of where to transport the goods, unlike our transporter of wood from the ship breaking yard who had no clue as to where he was going since he had never been south of Hyderabad.

The wife was called back and she kept rubbing it in. "I told you that I had a dream that a wrecking ball is going to come down on our house and you kept talking about some stupid mind/face reading skill."

I had no argument to counter this line of attack but only prayed that her dream would not come true.

Chapter 39

Suo Moto Stay

FIVE MONTHS WHIZZED by and demolition day (D-Day) arrived. The gates were barricaded, a line of cars was put against the gates and human chains were formed behind that. *Bhajans* were being chanted with all fervour, a *havan* was lit, women were crying and patriotic songs rendered the air.

On the other side of the gate was a large posse of policemen in riot gear, trucks of municipal workers with extra thick hammers and two bulldozers ready to break down the gates.

This almost resembled the Normandy invasion on D-Day from the movie 'The Longest Day'. Got an inkling of how it must have felt to be on the beach on that fateful day in 1944.

The press was having a field day with TV cameras from all channels beaming live pictures around the world. Better than the prime time legal debates.

The first day was a bit of a damp squib as nobody wanted to take the first step and it was obvious that the sympathies of the police force were with the residents of RRR and not with the smiling assassin's order.

The drama started in the same manner on the second day but after sometime the bulldozer operator got a bit bored or was recruited by the smirking seven/five star big builder and decided it was high time a gate was broken to allow the municipal workers inside the compound.

There was total pandemonium as they rushed in with their extra-large hammers eager to give vent to their frustrations by breaking down a few doors.

Reminded me of the time a chain snatcher got caught near the bus stop, and I, then a trainee doctor, was witness to the severe thrashing he received at the hands of all and sundry around the bus stop. I was later told by a consultant psychiatrist that the general public finds this to be the best way of venting all their daily frustrations out of their system and that they always keep an eye out for situations like this. Better than taking an anti-depression pill daily or visiting a shrink. Seems to be that the same logic was being followed by the municipal workers.

They were licking their lips and tightening their grip on the hammers, eagerly anticipating what was in store for them.

Suddenly, all demolition activity came to a standstill and you could hear people running around shouting "STAY", "STAY', "STAY".

What was going on? After all the 'King of Stays' was dead and there was no appeal for a stay pending in the Supreme Court.

But this was a 'Suo Moto Stay', being flashed on all the TV news channels. Whatever that means! Unheard of! A legal googly!

Martin Luther King in his famous speech delivered in 1963 on the steps of the Lincoln Memorial in Washington DC said "I have a dream."

The smiling assassin in the Supreme Court delivered an unusual speech, “I had a dream after watching the TV channels and I am granting a Suo Moto Stay for five months.”

Of course he did not mention, “I am retiring in four months, so this is not my headache anymore!”

The wife also had a wrecking ball dream which fortunately did not materialise and now she could return to Raven’s Nest to continue her dream house project.

PART 7

LAST TRIMESTER

THIS MEANS ONE has reached the home stretch and the morning sickness phase is over, life temporarily returns to normal and the pregnancy progresses smoothly.

Chapter 40

Roof Construction

Similarly, RRR was put on hold and Raven's Nest was looked at again. Since the money flow had started, it was time to tackle the interiors.

The wife had taken it upon herself to take charge of the interiors. Of course, she was left with no choice since the architect and contractor had raised their hands in surrender and said, "Madam, we are not experts in interior work."

Wise men!

They obviously were intimidated by the wife's friends who had periodically been visiting Kotagiri/Coonoor to keep her company while the shell was coming up. Listening to these ladies talk about various sophisticated interior plans, sourcing of artifacts from abroad and their general superior demeanor, left the simple hill folk befuddled. They felt it was wiser to retreat while they were still in madam's good books rather than get chewed up daily.

You have to give the devil its due. The Shell had come up very well and it was solid as it had faced several monsoons and been well cured. Some rooms were small, but that was more to do with our architect's fetish for *Vaastu*. But the crème de la crème was the roof.

I was very happy when the famous Mumbai architects had considered Kotagiri downmarket and found some or other excuse not to be involved in this project. Their mindset would have been that of a 'PLAINS' architect and they would have designed flat concrete roofs which are a big 'no no' in the hills. When one looks around, numerous new houses have mushroomed with such horrible flat roofs that I am sure the waterproofing company business will flourish in the hills as this is a guarantee for a leaking roof. It is possible that these same architects will soon buy a share in the water proofing companies. After all we are the fastest growing economy in the world and encourage such entrepreneurship.

Our roof resembled a typical old world British villa roof with symmetrical valleys, ridges and eaves. The roof was high and held up by solid rafters made of local wood and covered with interlocking red Mangalore tiles. This variety of tiles has been in use since 1860 when the German missionary Plebot set up the first tile factory in Mangalore. These tiles are solid as they are made from laterite clay and can withstand breakages even when the monkey brigade decides to use the roof as a playground.

The roof was held up by thick walls with wire cut bricks embedded in their outer surface. These wire cut bricks had a natural red brick colour that does not fade and were made by slicing a brick-sized piece from a bulk-length of clay with a wire tool. We had sourced the bricks from a factory in Kerala which unfortunately had perennial labour problems, resulting in an erratic supply. However, the quality was excellent and the red wire cut brick walls complemented the red Mangalore tiled roof to give the house an old colonial charm which contrasted splendidly with the surrounding lush green tea estate.

There was no water seepage through the roof as the wife had in no uncertain terms told our contractor that she was fed up with the leakages in Mumbai and did not want to see a spot of moisture on any of the walls. This may be one of the reasons why he personally spent several hours on the roof, supervising minutely how each tile was laid and was perhaps secretly pleased when it was subjected to the monkey test pre monsoons, lest he face madam's wrath post monsoons.

The wife was very pleased with the majestic roof and couldn't stop bragging about it to all her friends who visited. This pleased the contractor no end and he had made it a point to drop all other projects and be personally present when madam's Mumbai friends visited. A few months later after she had moved in temporarily, she was suddenly woken up, one night by a rattling noise on the roof just above her bed which kept her awake all night.

Next day, in a foul mood, she sent for the contractor and told him to immediately locate the fault. After spending a few hours on the roof, he told her that there was a small gap in the tiles through which some squirrels had entered and I suppose they were partying on the roof the night before. The wife blew her top and wanted to know why such a shoddy job had been done.

The poor chap did not have the nerve to say, "You wanted me to ensure there was no leakage, so

I performed the monkey test. You did not tell me you didn't want any noise, so I did not perform the squirrel test." When she was out of earshot, he quietly said to nobody in particular, "After all squirrels have been in this area long before this house was built and you are invading their habitat, so why don't you peacefully co-exist with them, madam?"

He never did surface again to hear her wax eloquently about the roof to her guests but found every excuse possible to avoid getting involved with the interiors!

Chapter 41

Interior Designer

NORMALLY, IT'S IN the interior work that the architects and contractors make the most money. It is a routine practice for them to get a commission from the suppliers of tiles, electrical appliances, and kitchenware or bathroom fixtures. Some architects also have interior designers (usually their kith and kin) working hand-in-glove with them and buy the most expensive paintings and furniture to enhance the beauty of the house. This helps in justifying the highly inflated bill presented to the hapless client.

Although they have been charged a bomb, most clients are thrilled as they have a 'designer' house. I suppose these architects, interior designers and contractors have attended a course in human psychology which unfortunately is not taken seriously by medical students since most doctors lack this skill of overcharging.

Any discerning visitor stepping foot in these 'designer' houses, after expressing the customary appreciation, would be secretly wondering why in the world house owners proudly display such garish items and then boast in a soft whisper about what it costs.

I suppose in this materialistic world money talks and the gaudier the display, the better.

The prime time TV drama of the RRR gate being defended and then later bulldozed down occurred on two or three occasions. Once it was cut short by the 'Suo Moto Stay' and once it was cut short by the 'Monsoon stay'. The latter as the name implies happened at the onset of the Mumbai monsoons.

Same scenario, except a different cast. An unscrupulous AOR whose main business was collecting commission threatened, insisting that an extra-large sum of money be wire transferred to his account in Delhi by 11am or else the very senior, reputed lawyer would not appear on our behalf at 3pm. You can imagine the trepidation this caused. All for a 'Monsoon stay'.

In the past senior surgeons made big incisions to operate and the complexity of the surgery was judged by the length of the scar. All that has changed now with robotic surgery popularising mini scars.

We seriously thought that the senior lawyer followed a similar adage (big surgeon-big incision; big lawyer-big charges)) and charged proportionate to his experience, little realising that this particular AOR was billing us in the lawyer's name but pocketing most of the money as his commission.

Fortunately, our architect and contractor did not fall into this category and they were happy to forgo all commissions, make less money but sleep with a clear conscience. Thus making extra money on the interiors was not on their agenda.

So the interiors, by default, fell into the wife's lap.

Chapter 42

Physiological Needs

The wife had become the chief interior designer and bottle washer. Sorry, the bottle washer tag came from a previous era and is not connected with this but I enjoy replaying it in my mind.

We had lived for over 14 years in USA and every time we were invited to a party, the husband of the house would pitch in with the cooking and cleaning of dishes. But in our household it was a bit different as I could not cook nor did I attempt to become an expert dish washer.

After every party the wife would stare at me and shout, "See how the other husbands help, do you think I am the cook and chief bottle washer?" This could be one of the reasons why she insisted on returning to India, to enjoy the good life.

In this case however, being the chief interior designer came with no perks but with hardships. I have to grudgingly admit that the wife overcame all these adversities and surpassed her job description.

Getting the interiors done while you are sitting in the same city is no mean feat as you have to coordinate the carpenter, plumber, mason, and electrician and see that the right design tiles, bathroom fittings, wood, etc. reach on time or else these guys will be happily twiddling their thumbs and charging you for it.

Imagine now, sitting in Mumbai and getting a house done in the Nilgiris which is over a thousand kilometers away, after the architect has thrown up his hands! This would seem to be an impossible task. So the only option was to move to the mountains as the mountains will not move to you. The wife did precisely that.

Coonoor is a one hour drive from the building site. The wife decided to move to Coonoor and set up base camp in her uncle's house since he spent most of his time in Bangalore and came to Coonoor only in summer. Her uncle, who had rejected the land initially due to its lack of view, had a house in a Coonoor tea estate which had been subdivided into plots where independent houses had been constructed. His was a charming three bedroom house with a lovely garden and a single pear tree which unfortunately attracted all varieties of monkeys who feasted on the tasty pears, leaving none for the inhabitants of the house. This helped in convincing the wife that she would not have any fruit trees in her new homestay as she was keen on attracting the human variety of guests rather than the animal variety.

Every morning she had to leave Coonoor with a packed sandwich lunch, take a cab, spend the whole day on site and cab it back late in the evening to an empty house. Repeating this routine daily can get tedious. But she did it with gusto.

The normal physiological functions of the human body involve frequent toilet breaks and this was a major problem in spending the whole day on site. Since her husband (that's me the great) insisted on all his patients drinking two to three liters of water a day, she followed suit. Depending only on the Coonoor house toilet did not seem practical as she would have been spending most of the day on the road going up and down for frequent toilet breaks, something akin to what the tennis players do when they are losing the game. The wife, obviously, could not use the fields like all the labourers were accustomed to, so the first priority was to get a temporary toilet built on site for her exclusive use. A practical solution to a vital problem.

The contractor was ordered to ready, before her return in a month, an outhouse for her use which could be later dismantled. On her return, to her utter surprise, she found that the contractor had over zealously built a well-planned solid bathroom a little distance away from the main house. He presented her with quite a fancy bill for his work of art. Furious at this excessive expenditure for a simple temporary bathroom, she shouted at him and wanted to know what he was thinking when he built this so-called piece of art. His reply was disarming, "Madam, when we built your roof, you said you didn't want any leakages in the house, so when I built the bathroom, I took all the precautions and used top quality material so that there won't be any leakages here."

The wife was stumped. Maybe it was wiser to just lump it and pay him the extra bit for his sincerity and good intentions. But she felt upset that this structure was finally going to be demolished as she could not have a bathroom sticking out like a sore thumb in the middle of the soon-to-be beautifully landscaped garden. Money down the drain!

On a future occasion when one of our architect friends from Mumbai visited and was walking round the perimeter of the house, he asked about this structure. We told him of our plans to demolish it as it had served its purpose as a temporary bathroom. After inspecting it, he realised a fair bit of money and effort had gone into it and he suggested that instead of destroying it, we should upgrade it. His argument was that with this lovely garden, guests would prefer to spend time outdoors and there may be lawn parties and if anyone needed to use the bathroom, they needn't enter the house but could use the readymade one in the garden.

So the contractor's sincere piece of work was upgraded, camouflaged with lovely plants and truly became a piece of art. Money, after all, didn't go down the drain.

Chapter 43

Cutting Wood

Now that her physiological needs had been taken care of, it was time for serious business. Since the wife had never done this sort of work before, nor was she a trained interior designer, she had banked on getting some help from the contractor and architect. But they had put up their hands in surrender and were relegated to the non-performing asset category (NPA). Thus she was basically on her own or more aptly put ‘up the creek without a paddle’.

Since the roof had already been done, she felt it would be wise to do the flooring next. Her logic was simple – start at both ends and work your way to the middle. She had hit upon this idea, the previous day after watching a father/son duo attack an extra-large masala dosa from both ends before reaching the central core.

She recruited a dozen carpenters from Mumbai who had done some work for her previously and made them camp inside the shell of the main house and told them to work at their own pace but get the flooring done without a flaw. She was sure they would work overtime and get the work done in the shortest possible time as these skilful carpenters were from Bihar where the temperature never goes below 45* degrees and here the temperature never goes above 22* degrees in summer. Since there was no heating in the house, they would be very keen to return to the warm confines of Mumbai rather than shiver in the cold Nilgiris when the temperature dipped to single digits in winter.

The first task was to cut the 'Manila Princess' twenty feet long strips of deck wood into smaller pieces, then plane it smooth before laying it on the floor. The contractor had told her that there was a saw mill in Kotagiri itself and the owner was willing to get the wood cut. The carpenters however rejected this approach as they felt they would be better off with an in-house sawing and planing machine. They would be able to cut the wood to the precise size required and would not have to worry about pilferages which were bound to happen in the saw mill. The wood after all was excellent quality, seasoned Burma teak and commanded a very high price outside.

How does one get a sawing cum planing machine? The NPAs had already thrown up their hands and their local saw mill friend feigned ignorance on the existence of such a combination machine as it meant a loss of business for him.

So the good wife did what she does best when confronted with a problem - pick up the phone and seek help from her husband's colleagues.

The husband had done his schooling in the Nilgiris and college education in Vellore. Vellore is synonymous with Christian Medical College (CMC), one of the premier medical colleges in India. Since Vellore town

does not offer much in terms of entertainment, the CMC group is a very tight knit community which spends most of its time in the hospital and the rest of the time in the hostel. This results in very close bonding and all a CMC graduate has to do is pick up the phone and ask another CMC colleague for help and rest assured it will be done, if possible. Something similar to the Italian Mafia, but in a more noble sense.

To reach Kotagiri, you have to fly into Coimbatore which is renowned for its engineering and medical institutions. Numerous ex-CMC doctors work in Coimbatore in very senior positions and all of them have patients in very diverse engineering industries. As seen earlier, doctors in India are still very well respected by their patients. All a doctor has to do is ask and a patient will move heaven and earth to oblige. Especially when he is explicitly told to help this special lady with all her household requirements.

Now the (NPAs) would not slow her down, as she had found a high value bond in the CMC connections which unlocked all the relevant doors in Coimbatore.

CHAPTER 44

BROKEN BLADES

THE SAWING CUM planing machine was finally located and transported to Kotagiri.

Here again the logistics problem came to the fore. All items had to be sourced from Coimbatore and sent up the hills, adding to the costs. No wonder building a house is more expensive and time-consuming in the hills. Many people, thus, find it less bothersome to just stay in a hotel or rent a room in a homestay while visiting the hills.

This has led to the popularity of homestays in the Nilgiris. The connectivity is good and the weather is great. Many of the homes resemble old British bungalows and we were keen that Raven's Nest finds a place in the elite category of homestays. To that end the interiors were important and the wife was determined to leave no stone unturned to achieve this goal.

The carpenters were thrilled to get a brand new sawing cum planing machine and did a small *puja* to inaugurate it. I realised that all the labour forces were big into religion as *pujas* are performed at the drop of a hat. Similarly, the liquor shop is also visited at the drop of a hat. I suppose both go hand in hand. Not being an overly religious person, I would prefer to hang my hat in the latter location.

Once the *puja* was over and the machine started working, the wife returned directly to Coonoor, unlike the husband who certainly would have taken a detour through the liquor shop just to celebrate the inauguration of the machine.

Happy after having achieved a major feat, the wife decided to sleep in late and check on the house only in the afternoon. She was shocked when she reached the construction site that afternoon. She had imagined the carpenters would be hard at work and the high-pitched sound of wood being sliced through the machine would greet her, but there was pin drop silence and all she could hear was the chirping of the birds. The machine lay idle and the carpenters were busy having their 'cuppa chai.' It almost looked like a sit down strike.

When questioned, they said that the cutting blade had broken in the night and so the machine had stopped working. When asked why they had not called to inform her, she got the standard answer that the cell phone was not working. Obviously their cell phone won't work if there is no money in the account, since hers was working perfectly well.

The problem was easily solved by calling up the Coimbatore supplier, explaining the problem and asking him to send up two more blades this time. Fortunately, numerous buses ply regularly between Coimbatore and Kotagiri and most of the bus drivers are willing to carry a small package for a nominal fee. Guaranteed delivery when the bus reaches the bus stand. Much cheaper and more efficient than FedEx or DHL. Four hours later the blades had arrived and all it had taken was just one phone call.

The wife gave the chief carpenter some money and ordered him to have the cell phone account in positive territory at all times and instructed him to call her immediately in case of any further problem. She left satisfied that a crisis had been averted and all would proceed smoothly from here.

On returning the next day, she was delighted to hear the buzzing sound of the wood passing through the machine. On reaching the house she was greeted by a beaming carpenter who earnestly told her that both the blades had broken again in the night and the first thing he had done in the morning was to call up the supplier and order six new blades.

The wife didn't have the heart to ask him why he had not called her up as instructed but instead had called the supplier directly. But she felt his initiative should not be questioned, lest next time he decided to call her up at midnight to report a subsequent problem. However, she did question him about his reason for ordering six blades when the two new ones and the first one had broken in such a short time. Obviously there was some underlying snag which was not being addressed and this cosmetic solution of ordering more blades was only going to inflate the costs without achieving the main goal of pinpointing the fault.

The next day, the wife, carpenter, broken blades and sample of wood that broke the blades went on a field trip to Coimbatore to try and crack this puzzle. Unfortunately, the machine was too large and heavy to fit into the cab and the supplier had promised to send a technician back if any further inspection needed to be carried out.

On reaching the Coimbatore office, the wife found it dark, stiflingly hot and was told that the air conditioners were not working due to the power cut. Coimbatore was facing a severe power outage and there were daily power cuts. Sitting in the dingy shop without an air conditioner was like baking in a pizza oven.

Something similar to the situation RRR faced when the power and water supply was cut following the court orders. People had to manage with emergency lamps and all windows open, hoping the cool sea breeze or monsoons would save them from the sweltering heat.

The wife yearned for her cool Kotagiri weather whereas the carpenter felt right at home and hoped the meeting would drag on so that his return to cold Kotagiri would be delayed. Two diametrically opposite thought processes on the weather but the common ground was both wanted the machine up and running.

The supplier had a look at the blades under a magnifying lens and assured the wife that they were all of good quality and there were no fault lines or manufacturing defects even though they were made in China. He was also flummoxed as to why these stainless steel blades were breaking so frequently. He crosschecked with the carpenter the exact machine settings being used and was reassured by the carpenter that he had used a similar machine several times before in Mumbai and the machine settings were as per the manual.

Just to tick off all the boxes in his inspection report, he finally reluctantly asked for a sample of the wood being certain that this would not be the cause of any problem, after all the job of this sophisticated machine was to cut wood.

When the wood piece was handed to him, he nearly fell off the chair. "Where on earth did you get this wood from?"

Well we got it from the sea! The wife explained the history behind the source and seasoning of the wood. He just laughed and his whole body relaxed. Like Archimedes, it was a Eureka moment!

He went on to explain that this well-seasoned extra thick Burma teak wood needed an extra tough blade to slice it and the blades which are routinely used for the normal logs would fall along the wayside like nine pins. We sure had ordered nine blades by now.

He was good enough to take the unbroken blades back, charge us a very nominal fee for the broken ones and gave us six new toughened blades which he felt would do the job. His only request was to leave the piece of wood with him as a souvenir as he had never seen such high quality wood before. So a piece of 'Manila Princess' sits in the supplier's showcase in Coimbatore while a large part of it forms the floor in Raven's Nest.

The carpenter was now keen to return and didn't think twice about returning to the cold Kotagiri weather. The wife, of course, was on the same page as far as the weather went. Both were eager to see how the sawing cum planing machine would perform with the new toughened blades. Something new to look forward to. Lesson 101 in interior design appeared to have crossed some major hurdles and was back on track.

Chapter 45

Double Quantity

The new blades worked like a charm and it was like slicing through butter. The floor boards were twenty feet long and four inches thick. The machine cut so precisely that the same thickness was maintained all along the twenty feet length. On seeing the accuracy of the machine's cutting ability, the carpenter, like the supplier, had a Eureka moment.

He felt that since each board was four inches thick, he would be able to split it in two long pieces of two inches thickness each and get two full length floor boards instead of one as earlier envisioned. Basically, double the quantity of wood available for flooring or two for the price of one. Another *'paisa vasool'* moment. In this way we would get enough wood to floor the whole house including all the bedrooms. In our earlier calculations, we felt the bedrooms in one half of the house would not have wooden flooring.

The left over extra small shavings of wood were used for the side skirtings on the floor and for the slats on the cupboards. Thus every square inch of wood was used.

The finished product looked very classy as the deep dark grains in the wood stood out against the plush brown background reinforcing the high quality of this well-seasoned Burma teak wood.

Getting an in house sawing cum planing machine paid rich dividends as we were able to double our quantity of available wood from the same volume. If we had given it to the local saw mill, we would have got only half the quantity from the same volume as a fair amount would have conveniently got mixed up with the other wood lying in the saw mill and got sold to someone else.

The supplier was also willing to take back the machine for half the price after we had completed all the wood work. I suppose my doctor friend in Coimbatore had really done some successful major surgery on the supplier's family member.

Three cheers to the college bond.

Chapter 46

Bathroom Tiles

Now that the wood flooring work was progressing satisfactorily, the wife turned her attention to the bathroom tiling. Since the house had six bedrooms, there would be six bathrooms attached to the bedrooms and two to the dining areas making a grand total of eight indoor bathrooms to be tiled.

This was a major project as along with the tiling, the bathroom fixtures and plumbing would need to be fixed. Ordering bathroom fixtures for eight bathrooms takes some doing as one has to color coordinate the fixtures to the tiles.

The wife, on one of her early literary festival trips to Jaipur, had visited a hand-painted tile shop and the vibrant colors with the varied patterns on the tiles had caught her fancy. In a flash she had decided that if she ever built a house, she would procure these tiles from Jaipur. On her return she shared this exciting piece of news with me and I dutifully shook my head in agreement at all the appropriate moments during her monologue. Having lived with her for so long, I did not pay much attention to this gibberish as I was confident that this idea would be replaced by a new one when she returned from her next literary sojourn.

But for once I had misjudged her intentions and when we decided to build Raven's Nest, she called up her contacts in Jaipur and told them to locate the actual factory where these tiles were manufactured as she wanted to go to the source and not the outlet. Something akin to getting the wood from the actual ship and not the bazaar.

Once the source was located, she didn't wait for the next literary festival but took the earliest flight to Jaipur. Her motto was one cannot combine work with pleasure. So the serious business of choosing tiles cannot be clubbed with a relaxing evening on the lawns of Diggi palace listening to a renowned author hold forth on the latest Pulitzer Prize winning novel. I, on the other hand, always combined work with pleasure since at all medical conferences we spend as little time as possible in the lecture halls and chill in the liquor halls discussing all subjects other than medicine.

The wife must have had some premonition that her new house would have six attached bathrooms even before we had frozen the design plans as she bought these hand-painted tiles in three different colours – blue, yellow and pink. After the fiasco with the wood transport driver's knowledge of geography, she decided to have the tiles shipped to Mumbai and not to Kotagiri. She was worried that the Jaipur guy who was in the business of only exporting tiles may inadvertently ship them to Kota Kinabalu as he definitely would not have heard of Kotagiri.

The tiles reached Mumbai safely and she, very proudly, showed me the Jaipur loot. I must admit the tiles were very classy and had a distinct artistic pattern which stood out. Each of the three different coloured tiles, pink, yellow and blue had different floral patterns. The wife had outdone herself once again. Ignoring my compliments lest they disturb her thought process, she said that she now had to concentrate on color coordinating the bedrooms.

Her plan, which I figured out much later, was that since there were three distinct colors of bathroom tiles, she would match the bedrooms, curtains and linen with the same colors in order to make it easier for the domestic help to understand which bedroom she was referring to when she dished out her orders for getting a particular room ready.

In our earlier stint in USA, the wife had worked as a TV news producer in two of the major news affiliates of NBC and ABC. While producing the newscasts, they had been instructed that since this was being beamed to small town mid-USA, the content had to be dumbed down so that even a fifth standard student would understand it.

This was the logic behind her colour coordinated rooms as she figured our fifth standard failed domestic help needed to understand her instructions without her having to repeat them ten times. Since the house had two wings, one for the guests and one for us, the bedrooms/bathrooms/linen would henceforth be referred to by their color. Pink, blue and yellow either in the guest wing or our wing. Thus, guest yellow would indicate the yellow coloured room on the guest side and similarly, yellow ours would mean the yellow room on our side.

This would not require a genius to comprehend and since no genius would volunteer for the job of domestic helper, her interaction with the house help should be hassle free unless they were colour blind in which case she would have had to revert to the standard boring practice of numbering the rooms.

Fortunately, none of the domestic helpers had to be sacked for being colour blind. Surely, this would have resulted in a lawsuit for discrimination in USA.

As doctors in USA we had been warned that every patient has to be treated as a potential lawsuit. I hope that a similar situation does not arise in India where we are warned that every domestic helper you hire is a potential lawsuit. In that case many will join the Syrian refugees in a mass migration movement to Europe.

Now that the tiling colour coordination problem had been resolved, she needed to locate the tiling experts.

Chapter 47

Sudden Roadblock

The Bihar carpenters had some distant cousins from Uttar Pradesh who had done tiling and masonry work along with them for flats in Mumbai. Since the wife was well aware of the high standards these carpenters maintained, she did not hesitate in asking them to contact their 'country cousins'.

Obviously, these two groups were not country cousins by birth since they did not speak the same dialect or come from the same region but had become cousins by profession since they had worked on several projects together for the same top architect in Mumbai. As the top architect continued using their services, the wife's gut feeling that she had struck pay dirt was strengthened.

She did strike pay dirt because the top architect who was stuck with a multimillion dollar project in the City of Gold was desperately trying to get this mason group over. But none of them had a passport, let alone a birth certificate, so at the moment they were sitting in a small, dingy room in Mumbai and contemplating returning to Uttar Pradesh.

Fortunately, you don't need a passport to travel from Mumbai to Kotagiri (as yet!) and living in a vast shell under a Mangalore tiled roof in Kotagiri was far better than being cramped up in a dingy Mumbai room. The only deterrent was the cool weather but the wife was happy as this would work in her favour and be an incentive for them to work hard, finish their tiling job fast and scoot before the cold winter set in.

Now a roadblock suddenly appeared.

The masons pointed out that the bathroom floor tiling work could not be started till the inlet/outlet pipes were laid and the wall tiling could not start till the electric lines were laid. So the wife asked them who was going to do that and they stared at her as though she had come from another planet and stated that it was obviously the work of a plumber and an electrician.

A very similar incredulous look had been given by the contractor at the beginning of the project when we had asked him the meaning of foundation, plinth, and shell. These labourers must have wondered how on earth we, ignorant city types, had become their bosses. That's how revolutions start. Fortunately we are a peace loving nation and people are more worried about where their next square meal is coming from than starting an uprising.

The NPAs' should have given the wife a basic class on the sequence of steps to be followed as this would have prevented such a blunder. Now that the masons had arrived with their cooking utensils and working tools, there was no way the wife could send them back. Unlike the old days when letters delivered at the wrong address were sent back with a sticker 'return to sender'.

She knew if she did this, they would find a job with another 'sender' and she would be left high and dry.

One often reads about landslides causing roadblocks but till one actually faces such a situation, one doesn't realise the helplessness of the position. On a recent road trip, we took, from Srinagar to Sonmarg, the steady stream of traffic on the narrow mountain road came to an abrupt stop. After waiting for several minutes, the driver walked forward and returned with the worrisome news that there was a landslide ahead and no one knew how long it would take to get it cleared. There was nothing one could do to rectify the situation and you felt powerless. At this point one had to take a calculated decision to either sit it out and wait or cut one's losses and turn back.

Being a smart lady, she was able to think laterally and was not stuck solely with tunnel vision. She felt now that the masons were a captive audience, she might as well put them to work on tiling the verandah and keep them occupied till she figured out a way to solve the electrician/plumber dilemma.

An SOS was sent to all her architect contacts in Mumbai asking them to send a plumber/electrician to Kotagiri ASAP.

When the court ordered the electricity and water to be cut for the 'illegal' higher floors in RRR, the municipal authorities were clueless as to how to do this without jeopardising the connections to the lower five 'legal' floors. Each building had its own unique internal water connections and the electric wires were dangling haphazardly. It was only the local building plumber/electrician who knew his way around this labyrinth and his assistance was much in demand.

Lessons are always learnt the hard way. The Mumbai architects wisely suggested that she find a local plumber/electrician to do the work as whenever any minor problem was encountered in the future, the local plumbers would otherwise just throw up their hands and ask her to call her Mumbai specialist plumber who had laid these pipes.

A similar situation arises when patients go abroad for surgery and spend huge sums of money for a procedure which could quite easily have been done locally. When they run into a problem down the road, the local surgeon usually throws up his hands and tells them to return to their operating surgeon for advice since he is the person who knows what was done inside the body.

Similarly, when a fly by night surgeon comes from abroad and operates on a patient here during a workshop, if some complication occurs, the local doctors will throw up their hands and say it is not their job to deal with someone else's complications.

This is a practical problem which, most people do not realise, may occur when you get outside experts to help for a situation which can be tackled locally.

Where could the wife get a competent local plumber/ electrician? All her high level contacts were in Mumbai and they had conveniently washed their hands off the task and told her to look locally. Who was she going to contact locally?

Chapter 48

Eavesdropping Driver

It so happened that the taxi driver knew a spattering of English and he always enjoyed listening to Madam's talks on her cell phone as she seemed to be talking to important people all the time and it helped him improve his English.

When the wife disconnected the phone and before she could start her next phone dialogue, he quietly chipped in, "Madam, our taxi company also owns an electric/ plumbing company and we have done many houses here. When I am not driving the taxi, I go and help the electrician as our Sir wants us to be good all-rounder's."

Talk about multitasking! Maybe some of our city MBAs' (Master of Business Administration) should come and do an internship here.

Wow, strutting around with an iPhone glued to your ears and talking nonstop seems to have some benefits although the eavesdropping bit can be a bit worrisome.

The wife, being a workaholic, told the driver to get her a list of clients whose houses they had worked on and then she planned to visit these clients and see for herself the quality of the work done before going and meeting the multitasking Sir.

Having completed the client survey in record time and satisfied with what she saw, she told multitasking Sir to put his boys on the job immediately. Sir was shocked. He had never met such an assertive woman who did not speak about a budget or ask for an estimate. He was used to the local crowd who bargained and bargained before going to his rival to try and get a lower price.

He assumed that she must be some hotshot interior designer from Mumbai who had no time for such mundane issues like budgets as she had several projects going on in different parts of the country.

Little did he know that this was her first project and the reason she had not haggled about the price was that she had a houseful of masons whom she needed to get on the main track: the bathrooms rather than allow them to work on the side tracks: the verandahs.

I got a frantic call the next day from the wife and was ordered to buy her a car in Coonoor. She did not want to take a taxi anymore as all the drivers eavesdropped on her personal conversations and she could not put up with such nonsense.

I wanted to ask, "Who asked you to keep yakking all the time on the phone and didn't this eavesdropping help in solving the electrician/plumber problem?" But of course this was only my thought process. Could not afford to openly say this and get shouted at again even though I was a thousand kilometers away.

A car was bought. A non-English speaking driver was hired. The driver never imagined that not knowing English would be an advantage! Taxi service discontinued.

Multitasking Sir was not unhappy as the taxi contract was replaced by an electrical/plumbing contract.

CHAPTER 49

ARCHITECT'S SOLUTION

THE ELECTRICIAN/PLUMBERS ARRIVED with their pipes and wires and started hammering on the walls and bathroom floor.

The famous Bert Lance 1977 saying 'If it ain't broke, don't fix it' obviously had no meaning here as the foundation and plinth had to be broken to get the inlet/outlet pipes through to the bathroom and the walls of the various rooms had to be chipped to lay the electric wires.

The wife was very depressed to see work that had been done by one group now being undone by another group but had to lump the explanation that was how it was done. She was determined that when she got back to Mumbai she was going to sit with her architect friends and discuss this point of building, breaking and re-plastering. If necessary tell them that when they were teaching young architects the trade they should emphasise more on teaching them to plan the execution of the layout properly at the drawing stage, so that such wasteful practices would be eliminated.

Noble thoughts but who will want to change their set ways is the question.

The electrician kept nagging her to decide on where she wanted the light and plug connections so that he could start laying the wires. This irritated her to no end as only the shell was up and she wondered how anyone could at this early stage, expected her to decide on where the lights should be placed when this depended more on the furniture arrangement and she had not even thought about what sort of furniture she would buy.

In the meantime the masons kept complaining that all the workers were walking on the verandah and damaging their tile work there.

The carpenters wanted to know whether they could start building the bedroom cupboards or if they needed to wait for the electrical work to get over.

The plumbers kept calling her back to the bathroom to ask her about the position of the sink and commode and what type of fittings were going to be used.

This was a very frustrating period and it appeared as if the wife had lost control and everyone was working at cross purposes. She even went to the extent of calling me and pouring out her frustrations.

I, who was only accustomed to listening to her firings and maintaining a studied silence, suddenly realised that she was actually asking for my emotional support and I was expected to say something caring. Basically, it was supposed to be a two way conversation not the usual monologue and I was completely out of my depth.

I quickly got my wits about me and said that I would be there by her side in this time of need.

My physically going there was not going to be of much use as I was even more clueless than her. So I did the next best thing, got a very good architect friend of ours to take the next flight there.

His mandate was to go there and do the firefighting. Sit with all the different workers and streamline the schedule so that all the work progressed methodically in one direction. He was able to do this seamlessly in a very short time and the wife was relieved. She could finally put up her feet and relax and let the work continue on auto pilot.

Besides keeping tabs on the aesthetics, her only job now was to act as an interpreter amongst the workers as the plumber/electrician spoke Tamil, the carpenter/mason spoke Hindi and some outside labour spoke Kannada. The ex-taxi driver who was now the electrician's sidekick continued with his smattering of English which had now started going downhill as he had no opportunity to eavesdrop on Madam's cellphone calls.

The non-English speaking driver she had hired cheerfully drove her down to Coimbatore on several occasions when she had to pick up the indoor fittings. After the initial hiccoughs with the traffic lights, these trips soon resembled a Prabhadevi-Colaba drive as she was continuously on the phone with no worry of her conversation being understood by the driver.

CHAPTER 50
DROP DEAD

SINCE OUR ARCHITECT friend had laid out the broad roadmap, all the pieces of the jigsaw puzzle gradually fell into place and the chief interior designer could breathe more freely.

As she had envisioned, the country cousins were in a tearing hurry to complete the work and like the 1970 TV wild west show 'Gun Smoke' they wanted to 'get the hell out of Dodge' before the winter set in. They used to hammer away late into the night and were not governed by society work rules as Raven's Nest was in the wilderness.

In RRR all internal individual flat work could start only after 9am and had to be finished by 7pm. During the period between 2pm and 4pm no work was allowed as this was siesta time for the occupants of other flats in RRR. Consequently it was a very short work day, as by the time the labourers arrived, it was already 11 am and it became a five hour work day with numerous chai breaks coupled with the afternoon work curfew. If by chance a labourer, by mistake hammered or used a

drill even five minutes past 2pm, the neighbours were ready to press the complaint button on their phones and the owner was usually hauled up for not having instructed his workers correctly.

No such curfew existed in Kotagiri and the workers could work till they dropped dead and nobody would have bothered.

In fact, one worker did die while at work.

He did not belong to the 'country cousin' gang but to the outside Kannada speaking gang. He must have been about seventy years old, but looked eighty and was on numerous medications. In USA, he would have been declared 'unfit to work' and would have been sitting at home collecting his government dole.

But in India since there is no government dole, he had to work for his daily bread.

One day, he forgot to take his medicines as he had spent all his money in the nearby liquor (Brandy) shop the previous night and had not been smart enough to call in sick that morning. He came to work with a tremendous hangover and was giddy and unsteady on his feet, due to lack of medication.

A large pit had been dug in the garden as this was to be the future home of the septic tank. While walking past it, our giddy friend lost his balance and went head first into the pit. Fortunately it was empty; otherwise you can imagine the stink it would have created!

After much difficulty he was extracted from the pit. Shaken and staggering on his feet, he was taken to a nearby hospital where he promptly fell asleep. Since there were no fancy imaging machines there, the doctor after listening to the history, presumed he was in deep post alcoholic slumber as his vital parameters were normal, there was no obvious bleeding wound and he had come walking to the hospital.

So he was left to sleep on an empty bed with the instructions that the doctor would re-examine him the next day once the alcohol was out of his system. Unfortunately, when the doctor arrived next day, he realised that our giddy friend had not been asleep in an alcoholic slumber but had suffered a brain injury which had taken its toll during the night and sadly this patient was definitely not going to wake up again.

The wife who had missed all this drama the previous day as she had been on one of her household shopping jaunts to Coimbatore, arrived at a deserted work site. She had visions of all the labour having suddenly decided to decamp but her fears were put to rest by the sole watchman on the site who brought her up to speed on the events of the previous day.

All the labour had gone to attend the funeral of the late giddy man.

The wife panicked imagining a million $$$ lawsuit staring her in the face as the labourer had died on the worksite and this would be the fate facing any landlord in USA. Her apprehensions soon vanished as her non-English speaking driver was quite calm about the situation and said that now all the evil had been removed from this house.

The local belief was that with his death, the giddy man had held on to all the evil around this house and now taken it with him through the dark hole. The driver seemed to be very knowledgeable as he belonged to the giddy man's tribe and this was a common superstition amongst them. He went on to say that all the wife had to now do was to hire the late giddy man's wife to work for her and pay for all the funeral expenses which would also include a large liquor bill as the next stop after the burial ground would be the liquor shop.

Since the driver was also keen to attend the funeral, the wife decided to take a taxi home as she was convinced that after the burial customs were over the driver would be eagerly looking forward to partaking in part two of the ceremony. Since he had saved her the stress over a million $$$ lawsuit, his attending any part of the funeral and even calling in sick the next day was his prerogative.

Chapter 51

Electrical Inspection

While the electricians were going about their merry job of laying yards and yards of high quality cables, news spread like wild fire that a homestay in the Nilgiris had been raided by the Electricity Vigilance Team and charged a phenomenal fine. To escape the fine, the homestay had decided to shut shop.

Information gradually trickled down that all homestays were required to have a separate commercial electric line connection for the guest wing and a domestic electric line connection for the personal wing. This rule was written in very fine print is some vague notification which had been issued several years ago and nobody had paid heed to it or complied with it. It had been buried in some obscure government office.

In the RRR battle, a big builder wanted to build a five star hotel on the adjacent plot of land and when he was denied permission because of the pending legal case involving RRR, he intervened and moved the case along at an extremely fast pace.

In the Nilgiris, the hoteliers were hurting because a lot of tourists preferred the homely, cozy atmosphere of homestays to the formal ambiance of hotels.

Rumor has it that a few of the hoteliers, pulled out the rule book and lobbied hard to see that the authorities follow all that was written in fine print. In this way they felt many homestays would have to close down as these are basically Mom and Pop joints with shoe string budgets that would not be able to pay the higher commercial electricity rates or the heavy fines imposed if they failed to comply.

The moral of the story is that one should never mess with the hotel lobby or builder lobby that wants to build hotels!

Since our house was still in the shell stage and the electricians were busy chipping away at the wall to lay their high quality cables, we had the liberty of changing course midstream. The wife quickly assessed the pros and cons and decided that we should be fully compliant with all the laws so that we don't face any problem in future as was happening in RRR.

The electricians were instructed to keep two separate lines and use only commercial electricity for the guest side. They felt this could be easily accomplished at this stage since no permanent connections had been installed and it would be feasible to get two separate electric meters.

The wife's wise decision was bang on. Several years later when the homestay was up and running, she had an unannounced team of five visitors who flashed their badges and said that they were from the Electricity Vigilance Board and since she was running a homestay they needed to conduct a surprise check.

They were the ones in for a surprise as she nonchalantly continued reading her book and told the domestic help to show them the guest wing. Without a hint of panic she told them to take their time and do a thorough inspection. She also told them that once they had finished, they could partake of some homemade cake and tea which she would keep ready for them as she was now in the hospitality business. They had never before faced such a cool customer!

After completing their inspection, they complimented the wife for being so meticulously compliant with the law and such a gracious hostess. They admitted that they had very rarely encountered such hospitality at other homestays, where often their visit had ended unpleasantly with them levying heavy fines on the owners and obviously never being offered a glass of water, let alone a cup of tea and delicious cakes.

In RRR when the authorities came to cut the power lines and went into the electric meter rooms, they happily invited all the TV channels into the room as this was their moment of glory and they did not want to miss out on a chance of being on live TV. Once they entered these meter rooms, they realised the wires were placed in such a haphazard manner that their task was going to be challenging without the help of the local electricians, so they quietly told the TV channels to leave citing the possibility of an electric fire when the wires were cut.

On the other hand, the electricians in Raven's Nest had done such a great job and all the meters were arranged so symmetrically, that the authorities would have been proud inviting the TV channels to watch the wire cutting ceremony.

Unfortunately, this was not to be as we had complied with all the fine print and were completely legal.

Chapter 52

Working Fireplace

One of the advantages of building a house in the Nilgiris is that there is no need for air conditioning as it is cool right through the year. This is a major expense avoided. But on a cold winter night, sitting around a nice warm fire, sipping a drink and chatting with friends would be something to cherish. So a fireplace in the middle of the sitting room had been on our initial wish list given to the architect. It is only after the shell had been constructed did we realise that it had joined the 'Missing in Action' casualty list as we saw no sign of the fireplace when we entered the shell.

The wife was most upset and planned to pin him down on this. However, on learning that the NPAs' had left her in the lurch with regard to the interiors, she had more on her plate to worry about than a stupid fireplace.

Now that the house was going on autopilot, thanks to our Mumbai architect's input, she had time to check out the social scene in Coonoor. Her reputation preceded her and the who's who of Coonoor were falling over each other to have her over (according to her words!). I wasn't buying this as I knew nobody in Coonoor had heard about her as they are quite content in their insulated lifestyle where an evening of bridge, rummy or bar night was the highpoint of their night life.

Some of the houses she visited on this party circuit had very ornamental fireplaces and after seeing these, she was inspired to revive her fireplace plan. Unfortunately, none of her hostesses had the actual fire burning during these parties and she wondered why. One day while attending an afternoon tea party the fireplace topic was brought up and most of the ladies were of the opinion that the fireplaces built in the newer houses were only ornamental in nature. Further probing revealed that many contractors did not know how to construct a functional fireplace and when the fire was lit the smoke bellowed into the sitting room instead of being sucked up through the chimney. But all these ladies were confident that some of the more experienced architects would have the know-how to overcome this flaw.

Although the NPAs' had washed their hands off the interior work, the wife was certain that they would not shy away from a challenge. She very sweetly told them that most of her friends were complaining of the poor fireplace designs and that she had boasted that her architect/contractor would surely be able to construct a perfectly functional fireplace. She had well and truly reeled them in and they had no avenue for escape.

Give the devil its due. Our architect spent several hours designing a perfect fireplace and supervised the construction at every step. The final result was fabulous and the smoke actually went up the chimney and did not smoke the guests out of the sitting room.

After seeing this functional fire place, several people actually contacted our architect and requested him to rectify theirs. But he had his hands full as madam would not release him now as she felt that even if he was not keen on the interiors, she could somehow persuade him to get involved in the environment friendly measures she had planned for the house. The NPAs' were after all experts in house construction as borne out by the high quality roof and fireplace they had built.

CHAPTER 53

ENVIRONMENTALLY FRIENDLY

NOW THAT THE title of NPA was defunct since they had returned to their original avatar of expert architect/contractor, the wife had to find them a challenging piece of work.

The whole world was concerned about climate change and the wife was determined that she would contribute her tiny miniscule effort to stem this rot by adopting as many environment- friendly measures as possible. She had a good lieutenant in our architect as he was also passionate about this subject.

Water is a precious commodity in the hills and while buying this property our tea factory friend had lectured us on the importance of having water on the land. We were keen to augment this with rain water harvesting.

In RRR, since the buildings were only supposed to be five storeys high as per the sanctioned plan, the amount of water supplied from the municipality was proportionately calculated. This water was inadequate for the whole building as several 'illegal' floors had supposedly been built. Some buildings had to depend

on tanker water to augment this meagre supply while the others dug bore wells and supplemented this stock by implementing rain water harvesting.

In a city like Mumbai with such heavy monsoon rainfall if more 'legal' buildings had also adopted rain water harvesting measures, this would have gone a long way in easing the perennial water cuts.

In Raven's Nest, the high roof with the numerous valleys and ridges had a large surface area and during the rains, torrents of water would gush down on all sides. The well placed Mangalore tiles prevented any leakage in the roof. The wife was keen to direct this bountiful supply of water into storage tanks and not just let the water go to waste.

She challenged the architect to design an aesthetic looking drainage system so that the whole house was not surrounded by ugly looking aluminum drainage pipes. He rose to the challenge and got the roof guttering done in a colour matching the red Mangalore tiles and instead of using solid pipes to drain the water down, he substituted them with stainless steel chains to act as a conduit for the water which was then filtered and stored in larger underground tanks.

He had seen this in a foreign architecture magazine and was sure that madam would approve of the design as it truly looked classy but was not sure she would approve of the price which was astronomical. He was in for a surprise as she lavished him with praise for his enterprise without once mentioning the cost overrun.

I suppose when it comes to environmental issues, cost is of no concern.

Incidentally, since the whole outer shell of the house was lined by red wire cut bricks, these did not require a yearly paint job as their natural brick color had a long shelf life. This was an environment-friendly measure, thought of much earlier, by the Madam and her new found architect lieutenant as they felt the noxious fumes of paint would pollute the pure Kotagiri air and should be avoided as far as possible.

The air in the Nilgiris is very pure and Kotagiri is rumored to have the purest air. All newcomers are constantly bombarded with the oft-repeated refrain that a person lives till the age of eighty in Ooty, ninety in Coonoor and has to be shot dead in Kotagiri!

The sun in the hills is very sharp and in summer if one spends a lot of time outdoors, patches of sunburn can develop on the exposed skin. This is one of the reasons why many people in the hills wear hats when they are in the fields. Must have learnt this from the British. Fortunately, the constant cool breeze makes working under a hot sun quite enjoyable.

Surprisingly in winter, the day time sun is also intense and once while driving past a church, we noticed some people on the roof wearing hats while fitting what appeared to be solar panels. On talking to them we learnt that the climate here is ideal for solar water heaters and one does not have to use traditional geysers to heat the water for a bath.

The newspapers were full of articles on India taking a lead in the global warming conferences and promoting solar energy as the way forward. The government also advertised various schemes to popularise setting up of solar lighting and heating systems in houses. But when you actually dug a little deeper, these advertisements had no credibility as setting up a solar water heating system or lining your driveway with solar lights is way more expensive than using the traditional methods.

But as I said earlier the motto in this house was that when it came to environmental issues, cost would be of no consequence.

The house was subsequently equipped with solar water heaters, the road with solar street lamps and the kitchen with solar cookers.

I must confess all the solar powered devices were top class.

The solar heated water was very hot and the only drawback was that everyone tended to take a longer bath as one didn't feel like getting out from under the shower. The solar street lights switched on automatically and burned bright at the first sign of darkness setting in and illuminated a large area around them. The food cooked in a solar cooker was extremely tasty and easy to prepare.

On realising how solar efficient the house was, the wife decided that all she needed in future, besides a large kitchen was an organic vegetable garden and before long she could run exclusive solar organic cooking classes in Raven's Nest.

This is what you call enterprise and putting solar energy to good use.

Chapter 54

Classy Kitchen

The kitchen was the wife's forte as she was an excellent cook. In fact she had tried to kick-start her journalism career by attempting to write a cookery book on Indian vegetarian cooking while single-handedly running a home and managing two kids in USA. Single-handedly because her husband (the great me) was too busy with his work or too lazy (your choice) to lift a finger around the house. My house program was feet up, TV on loud, beer in hand and a 'Do not disturb sign'. It actually used to work!

The book did not get published since it was the 1980's, the era of non-vegetarianism, pre IT boom when India was an unknown entity in USA so no publisher imagined that any reader would be interested in a book on vegetarian cooking let alone one authored by an Indian. So the project failed to take off.

But she was determined that her new project on organic solar cooking at Raven's Nest would take off and foreigners would flock to attend as organic, vegetarian food was very popular now and people were keen to visit India which was turning out to be a safe tourist destination. The added attraction of environmentally friendly solar cooking would attract the discerning crowd that would also enjoy yoga on the lawns and visit the heritage spots in the Nilgiris.

To achieve this goal she had to have an elegant, top class kitchen on par with those displayed in glossy Interior Design magazines. The easiest path would have been to get one of the pre-fabricated modular kitchens installed. Less headache, no supervision and a stress free option. But she decided to go about it the hard way by designing it and supervising every minute detail herself.

I would like to believe that her intention was based on the phrase 'the best way to a man's heart is through his food' but I am sure this thought never entered her mind and her sole aim was to get an efficient kitchen that mirrored her personality.

Having seen many modern kitchens in USA, she knew exactly what she wanted. A large island counter with several gas burners was the center piece of the kitchen. A powerful exhaust vent was placed strategically above the gas burners. To get this fixed at the correct height, required some engineering ingenuity as a separate wooden beam had to be drilled into the wall to hold this vent along with the surrounding canopy of lights. To an untrained eye this resembled a guillotine just waiting to fall and chop off the cook's head in case the person who secured the wooden beam had been a bit lax in his job. But knowing the wife's sharp eye for details, I think the cook would never have to worry about such an eventuality nor would the wife have to search for a replacement cook with an attached head!

Several wooden cabinets lined all the kitchen walls and their colorful handles added spice to the kitchen. Getting them made to specific proportions was no easy task, as the carpenters felt simple open shelves would serve the same purpose and building self-shutting magnetic doors just added to their work. The seasons were changing and they were in a hurry to leave before winter set in as they didn't possess any winter garments. They had never in their wildest dreams imagined a place in Tamil Nadu could be so cold as the farthest south they had come was to do some project for the Christian Medical College, Vellore in the height of summer when the temperature was in the mid 40 degrees. This influenced their perception that all of South India had a semi- desert temperature. So all the wife's persuasive powers were bought into play, to win the carpenters over to her line of thinking, as she wanted them to be fully committed while building the cabinets. A sweater gifted to each of them also played a small part in this change of mindset. Long live bribery.

To say the kitchen was spacious was an understatement. If a Mumbai broker had seen it, he would have readily put it up for sale as a studio apartment. This was the only non-*Vaastu* compliant room in the house. The wife had told the architect categorically in one of the early meetings as to how she wanted the kitchen shaped and although this did not gel with his *Vaastu* calculations, he wisely decided rather than argue with her that it would be better for the dominant *Vaastu* of the remainder of the house to overcome this non- *Vaastu* room. He had gathered after watching the interaction between the wife and husband as to who was the boss and he was well aware that in any discussion the boss is always right.

One of her Mumbai friends on hearing about the house construction project in the Nilgiris offered some advice as her father had worked for a British tea company in this area. Growing up in the hills, she vaguely remembered a special 'Nilgiri refrigerator' which kept vegetables and fruits fresh in the pre-refrigerator days and felt that this would be an added attraction in the house.

When the wife asked around, nobody seemed to have heard of this Nilgiri refrigerator. However, when she described the cupboard, our architect immediately knew what she was referring to. Like yoga which originated in India and was never patented, the Niligiri refrigerator has never been patented or popularised. Basically it is an open cupboard protruding through the wall in a north-south direction with a mesh covering on both sides. This allows the cool air to filter freely through the cupboard at the same time keeping out the sun, rain and insects. Food kept in this cupboard remains fresh for several days.

She had planned to incorporate a Nilgiri refrigerator in the extra-large kitchen and while the kitchen carpentry work was going on, she asked the architect about where it could be placed in the kitchen. She got a jolt when he told her that the wall would have to be broken to fit it in the correct north-south aligned direction. After weighing the pros and cons she realised that breaking and rebuilding is part of the game in house construction, similar to what she had seen with the pipes being brought out of the bathrooms by breaking the plinth.

Reluctantly, she agreed to have this done to the kitchen wall; all for a Nilgiri refrigerator which obviously was environmentally friendly and a unique addition to her kitchen.

The solar cookers presented no such placement problem as they were portable and could be kept in an empty corner and taken out during the day to do their magic in the sun. She had first seen them in use in Bhavnagar when she had gone to the Alang ship breaking yard to collect the wood. Her husband's patient, who assisted her in sourcing the wood, had a nice flat with a large balcony. Just before leaving for a day trip to inspect the wood, the wife had observed the lady of the house put some soaked rice, vegetables and dal in four black colored containers and leave them on the terrace inside this big box which she later learnt was a solar cooker. The sun did the rest and when they returned several hours later, dog tired and famished, lunch was ready. The food was piping hot and ready to be served straight from the solar cooker to the dining table. No marketing genius had to do a sales pitch; the wife was sold on the idea of using solar cookers and ordered a dozen. Most for herself and some to be given to her friends in Mumbai who had never imagined they can cook food without the famous gas connection.

During the RRR turmoil when the gas connections were disconnected, the wife led the ladies in using the building terrace to do their daily cooking by lending them her solar cookers and using the free sun shining over Mumbai. Some of them got so taken up by this simple contraption that even after the gas was restored, they continued cooking in their recently acquired solar cookers as they found this much cheaper and besides, it gave them the freedom to leave the house while the food was being cooked.

The kitchen was finally done to perfection. The carpenters and their country cousins started packing up their belongings which now included a brand new sweater. The Madam started dreaming of her new cooking project but realised that she would have to source organic vegetables for this to succeed.

CHAPTER 55

ORGANIC VEGETABLES

THE SOIL IN Kotagiri is very fertile and the land around Raven's Nest has an abundant supply of water as it sits in a valley. Remember the wife's uncle rejected the land because there was no view.

If Kansas is considered the wheat belt of USA, then Kotagiri should be considered the vegetable belt of South India. Trucks from this area daily ply down the Ghats carrying all the freshly grown garden vegetables to be auctioned in Mettupalayam at the foothills of the Nilgiris and then they are distributed to the rest of the region from there.

The wife always dreamt of having her own small vegetable patch and now with the cooking class bug biting her, it had to be organic. But how does one cultivate organic vegetables without any knowledge of this specialty. The local gardeners were only used to spraying chemicals and pesticides to get quick results, quite unaware of the toxic effects of this chemical residue in the food. The wife had often heard her husband remark that there must be a large amount of dangerous chemicals in the food we eat as cancer is getting more rampant.

They say fortune favours the brave, but in the wife's case fortune favoured her when she attended a party and that is why she is a party animal. At one of her new Coonoor acquaintance's party, her ears popped up when she heard an animated conversation on organic vegetables and a little while later was able to corner the speaker who happened to be an expert in this field. Thus, a party helped her to discover her organic lady and the bond got stronger because they discovered that their husbands had gone to the same school although decades apart.

The organic lady was quite enthusiastic about helping the wife to turn a small patch of garden organic and grow organic vegetables. The main resistance came from the gardener who felt this was a terrible waste of time and a loss-making proposition.

A small patch of land near the well, at the bottom of the field, was earmarked for this project. It was cleared of the tea bushes, soil dug up once again and then strewn with mustard and various lentil seeds. In a short time the plants started to grow and it soon resembled a beautiful yellow mustard field, only seen in movies shot in the foothills of the Himalayas. The fertilizers used were cow manure and a combination of garden compost and vegetable oils. This process helped in naturally enriching the soil that had been contaminated with pesticides and chemicals over several years. After repeating this process several times, we finally planted our first crop of organic cauliflower.

However, our gardener was thoroughly frustrated when he noticed all the crops in the surrounding gardens flourishing and his organic patch getting riddled with insects and the cauliflowers resembled moth-eaten pieces of cloth. He was itching to get his chemical pesticides and spray the whole patch. The organic lady kept smiling through it all and tried to explain to the gardener that the chemicals used to kill the pests in the surrounding farms would also kill him some day but the organic vegetables would add years to his life.

This cut no ice with him as he felt that there was no use living for several years when he was losing money every day trying this stupid organic method. Fortunately, the money was not going from his pocket or else we may have been faced with a farmer's suicide. The wife who was paying for this whole exercise was quite willing to wait it out as she knew that ultimately the benefits would trounce the costs and all she had to do was mollycoddle the gardener and reassure him this was only a one year trial period and then they would revert to the standard chemical method if this did not work within that time.

She was quite sure it would work as the organic lady had said so and her organic cooking class was going to succeed. The power of positive thinking always helps.

CHAPTER 56

ART GALLERY

THE CARPENTERS AND their country cousins bid the grumpy gardener goodbye and left for the warmer shores of Mumbai after having done a terrific job which even the Madam could not fault.

The flooring was perfect and the tiling exquisite.

The wooden flooring was so warm and inviting that a person would prefer to remove their footwear and walk barefoot just to feel the smooth, seasoned wood under their feet. It definitely enhanced the character of the house and we had to thank our Mumbai ship owner friend for her brilliant idea and my ship breaking patient for helping us execute that idea.

The colour coordinated bedrooms with their Jaipur tiled bathrooms also added a unique touch to the interior of the house. Attending the Jaipur Literature Festival had some benefits after all.

The indoor lighting was enhanced by the custom made lamp shades specially ordered from a lamp shade boutique in Mumbai. The door handles and knobs were sourced from the person who supplies them to the Taj hotels but at a much more reasonable price. All these items were first collected in Mumbai and then trucked in a single container as transportation costs were high and they could not be sent piecemeal.

When the container arrived at Kotagiri there was a frenzy of activity as each item had to be fitted in the correct place. The wife literally had to be in two places at the same time. In Mumbai to oversee the loading, and subsequently in Kotagiri to ensure the proper placement. A tough task which she did cheerfully and only later did I realise that the container was also loaded with several paintings. These being the source of her overt enthusiasm.

The entire RRR drama was a sure shot precursor to depression especially if those genes ran in your family. The wife was aware of it, as depression was rampant in her family and one of the therapeutic remedies suggested by her party circuit friends was to follow the popular American TV series of the 1990's and 'shop till you drop'. She followed this advice to the hilt and during the RRR days went on an art collection binge.

I was totally unaware of both the depression and shopping angle until much later on. Her desire to be present at both the departure and arrival gates of the truck should have raised my curiosity, but being so immersed in my work, I neglected the urge to dig deeper.

A few months later when I was summoned to Raven's Nest to admire the interior work done by the wife, I noticed several paintings hanging on all the walls. The walls were literally crying under the weight of these paintings and there was not one free wall. The central painting which immediately caught one's eye was a depiction of a black bull on a deep red background by H.R. Dass. Classical paintings done by Jyoti Bhatt and T. Vaikuntam were placed above the music system on the other side of the room. The electric fuse box was hidden behind J.M.S. Mani's Badami series. A rare antique Tanjore painting hung above the fireplace. I had never seen these paintings before and when I politely asked her about the origin of these, she very nonchalantly announced that she had bought them at the various exhibitions that she regularly went to. On further questioning her about where they had been stored all these months, again, in a very matter of fact tone, I was told that they had been kept under our bed in Mumbai. Thank God we did not have an income tax raid for instead of bank notes stuffed in shoe boxes under the bed, the IT people would have come across hordes of paintings. With the price of paintings appreciating astronomically, I may have been hauled in to the cooler with a non bailable warrant!

But this would not have stopped the wife who would have gone about her merry way and continued adding to the pile of paintings unless of course she realised that there were no free walls inside the house to hang the paintings. Maybe she would have then found place outside.

CHAPTER 57

LANDSCAPE ARCHITECT

TALKING ABOUT OUTSIDE, what about landscaping? The beauty of a house goes up several notches if it is landscaped tastefully. The land being extra fertile in the Nilgiris, we noticed that most houses had beautiful gardens with a variety of flowers. The riot of colours was extremely pleasing to the eye. We were convinced that after having put in so much effort and money into the interiors, we needed to get an expert landscaper to complement this effort.

In Mumbai, the external appearance of most buildings is shabby as the societies don't have money to paint them regularly. Members are only interested in keeping their own flat posh and are reluctant to pay the society dues. In RRR, we were well aware of this problem of nonpayment of dues by society members; thanks to our exposure to the dirty dozen.

While renovating individual flats to make them look posh, any internal structural changes made need prior municipal permission. But if the municipality is unable to keep tabs at the building construction stage as in the

case of RRR, the question remains on how they would be able to monitor flat renovations.

Newer building complexes in Mumbai are now coming up with well-landscaped gardens and they advertise this fact proudly since builders have recently come to realise their importance in attracting the high net worth individuals. Additionally, thanks to the RRR saga, all these advertisements have a line mentioning the current status of the OC for that particular construction.

The Mumbai scene was ruled out as a potential source for locating a good landscape architect as most of the established ones had spent their lifetime becoming experts in construction/renovation and never had an opportunity to gain experience in landscaping due to the acute scarcity of space in Mumbai. The motto of 'may as well have a concrete livable structure rather than an open space' had been the dictum for many years although that was changing of late and the younger architects were experimenting with the concept of greenery in the newer complexes.

The meticulous wife was not keen on entrusting this work to any raw architect as she didn't want them to use her property as a research laboratory. She was well aware that in Bangalore all the old houses had well maintained gardens; hence Bangalore was often referred to as the 'Garden City'. She set her goal on recruiting a landscape architect from the garden city and decided to visit her uncle there and kill two birds with one stone.

Off she went to visit her favourite uncle who lived in Bangalore and whose house in Coonoor had been her base camp, while she had taken on the mantle of chief interior designer. Her uncle knew of a young architect who had just returned from Australia and had done an outstanding job landscaping the golf course. Since her uncle was a golf addict, he was very impressed with this young man's design and strongly recommended him for the project.

At first the wife was a bit skeptical as this was the same uncle who had rejected the Kotagiri land since it didn't have a view. But seeing how adamant he was and knowing first hand that he, a keen gardener, maintained a lovely garden in Coonoor, decided to take a gamble. She went ahead and asked the young architect to visit Raven's Nest and then show her what he planned to do. After all if the plans did not suit her taste, she could always tell him to return to his Bangalore golf course.

I wasn't bothered about what plan he would come up with as long as it included a waterfall.

A very good banker friend of mine who had built his dream house in Lonavala had told me several years ago that no matter what I built, I should make sure that there was a waterfall. He had told me this while we were sitting on his deck, sipping our drinks and listening to the pleasing sound of the water gushing. He mentioned that this was the sound he enjoyed listening to as it was so relaxing and all his worries of bad loans and NPAs (not connected to our Kotagiri NPAs') just vanished. Then and there I had decided that a waterfall was a must as it would help in mentally blocking the RRR worries.

The architect spent two days camping on site just to get the feel of the land and soak in the atmosphere. This, he said, always inspired him and generated a host of ideas which then needed to be transferred on to the drawing board on his return to his studio home.

On his first night there, to his utter shock, he saw some wild pigs running through the tea bushes. Very excitedly, next day he announced that from where he came, pork curry was a delicacy and since their tribe is allowed to possess guns, no wild pig would ever be able to run around free on an estate. He was willing to bring his gun along to get rid of them on his next visit and happily take the pork home. Unfortunately, the laws are such in Tamil Nadu and most parts of India that you cannot kill wild animals unless they are declared vermin. So the young architect had to return to Bangalore to draw up the landscaping plans minus the pork curry.

Chapter 58

Terraced Garden

In the olden days, architects would sit on their desks and draw their designs by hand and this would take much time. Our young architect depended on his computer and within seventy two hours sent us five different sets of designs. Modern technology had dramatically altered the scenario and now the ball was in our court to choose the appropriate design.

Since he had incorporated a waterfall in all the designs, my input was redundant and I left it all in the wife's hands. As you will realise, I have this fatalistic attitude and leave everything to God (wife in my case)!

Once the design was frozen, the estimate was calculated and that is when I realised landscaping costs a bomb. No wonder the Mumbai builders avoided these extra expenses as they get paid only for every square foot area of the flat sold and not for the garden in the building.

Our architect was not keen on using the local labour as he was well aware of their Monday morning blues which resulted in the extra-long curing process for the house. He said that he would send his team from Bangalore and they would camp in the grounds and work continuously. A few days later six stalwarts arrived but to our surprise they spoke a very strange language which none of us could understand.

One of the reasons I was keen on building a home in the Nilgiris was that I had done my schooling here at Lawrence School, Lovedale. This is a premier educational institution established in 1858 with stately, imposing buildings set in a lush campus of over seven hundred and fifty acres. Some of the labour used to construct these majestic buildings was Chinese prisoners rounded up during the opium wars in China and incarcerated in the Nilgiris.

In school we used to get Chinese tokens weekly in lieu of money and this could be exchanged for goodies in the tuck shop. Apparently, this Chinese money came from these Chinese prisoners and it is a pity that we did not preserve these coins as now they may have fetched a premium as antique coins.

Our school was constructed by Chinese labour and the strange language being spoken by our landscaping labourers turned out to be Bangla implying that the landscaping in Raven's Nest was done by Bangladeshi labour. Unlike the Chinese who were prisoners, our Bangladeshis had come to Bangalore of their own free will and were now camping in Raven's Nest. I never did get a chance to ask our young architect as to how or why he recruited these stalwarts.

The basic landscaping was completed in a relatively short time as these stalwarts worked for long hours without many breaks or visits to the local liquor den. The final product which was a three layer terraced patch with a multilevel waterfall and a deck jutting out above the tea bushes had great potential and would definitely enhance the overall beauty of the property once the flowering plants bloomed.

We were fortunate to recruit an enthusiastic gardener who came highly recommended, after having spent several decades working for a foreign lady who had taught him all the intricacies of gardening but unfortunately not the names of the various flowers. Since she had sadly just returned to UK in a coffin, our gardener was footloose and fancy free, searching for a job. We felt that this was an apt moment to let him loose in this recently landscaped, barren area and give him an opportunity to work his magic.

He sure did have a green thumb and was extremely passionate about his work. He first filled the three layer terraced area with square blocks of grass which he had dug up from the surrounding empty meadows that were used as a community cow grazing area by the local villagers. He brushed aside our concerns and said the grass would grow back in the meadow once the rains came and there was plenty of grass there at present, to feed the cows. He spent all his spare time watering and patting down these grass blocks to ultimately produce a lovely, green terraced lawn which resembled a rolled out carpet comparable to a golf putting green.

He planted pink geraniums and hollyhocks along with the orange dahlias in the flower beds which he then barricaded by constructing a lovely white wooden picket fence giving it a vibrant contrast of colours. He then put a few more rocks inside multilevel water fall so that the sound of the gushing water was amplified and lined the edges of the waterfall with white datura interspersed with a different variety of red dahlias and a few purple geranium.

Our green thumb gardener had transformed this landscaped area into a beautiful English garden and I am sure his former employer sitting in heaven would have been proud of his accomplishment.

CHAPTER 59

FINAL CONNECTIVITY

NOW THAT THE house and landscaping was complete, the only task left was the question of final connectivity. The roads in the Nilgiris were top class and one could drive comfortably from Coimbatore airport to the gate of Raven's Nest in two hours.

I am not a computer geek. My reference to final connectivity has nothing to do with computers or internet but to the final two hundred and fifty meters from our imposing black iron gate to the portico of the house.

Since this was an estate house, I wanted to leave it as an estate road. If you owned an SUV, then you would enjoy driving the last two hundred and fifty meters using a four wheel drive and getting the maximum thrill from off road driving. However, if you owned a regular car, then best of luck to you. It may be wiser to park near the gate and get your thrill of aerobic exercise by walking up the steep slope from the gate to the portico.

The wife dismissed my stupid hare-brained idea outright without even a second's deliberation and I was not surprised as by now I was well aware of what she thought of my mental acumen.

Her argument was that since the roads are so good in the Nilgiris, most people wouldn't want to be riding in an uncomfortable SUV but would rather use a regular car as there is no necessity to own a four wheel drive. If our final connectivity is poor, friends would be reluctant to visit once the first mandatory house warming party was over and done with. I was not concerned about her friends not wanting to visit, but her argument was sound and my selfish desire to own a top class SUV was crushed effortlessly.

I just realised that until now I have not introduced you to our trusted local Jeeves. Running around to get permits from the various government departments is a herculean task and fortunately the tea factory owner besides helping us to buy the property introduced us to his trusted Jeeves who was basically a man for all seasons. If there was any permit required, Jeeves was on top of it and confidently promised to get it within the next week. After some time we realised that Jeeves' week had way more than seven days but he had the street smarts to get the work done. This saved us a lot of heartburn and headache.

To match the quality of the local roads, we decided to use all the local road building equipment and expertise. To obtain this, numerous permissions are required and we decided it would be best to leave the road construction work in the able hands of Jeeves. Even if he got a little commission from the road contractor, it would not bother us, as long as the quality of the road was first-rate.

In Mumbai, yearly scandals of potholed roads and contractors fleecing the authorities with their substandard

road material, makes headlines during the monsoons and then is promptly forgotten till the next monsoon. The enquiry panels make some recommendations which are never followed and the same nexus is back in action the following year. It is a re-run of the same movie and the public seems to have gotten used to it since no political party has the will to change this. However, a recent change in government has shaken up the whole establishment as the new Chief Minister is all gung ho to root out corruption and what better place to start than the authority/contractor nexus. I wish he had been there when the authority/builder nexus was active in RRR three decades ago.

Our Jeeves took his job seriously and visited the site daily to ensure that the road was being made according to the stringent specifications laid down in the USA guide to road building. After all in USA, the interstate highways whose construction started in 1956 and now covers about fifty thousand miles have stood the test of time. Extreme climatic changes or the heavy vehicular traffic has not damaged these roads and they still remain in pristine condition and do not resemble the craters on the moon as the Mumbai roads do at the end of every monsoon.

The contractor took his time in building the road as he was following all the multilayer specifications diligently and he was so confident with the end product that he told Jeeves that he was willing to give a ten year guarantee.

This contractor would not be welcome with the road mafia in Mumbai as come every monsoon they need to earn money. If this person's roads last ten years, then their business would be jeopardised. The road mafia always supports the political party that restricts jobs

to these crooks ensuring that such competent outsiders will not be allowed in.

Jeeves was extremely proud of the job done by his contractor friend and we were very appreciative of Jeeves for meticulously supervising every square meter of the road construction. Friends who visited later lavished fulsome praise on the quality of the road which by now was fully shaded by the white alder and red spathodea trees which had been planted well before the house construction had started and was now home to a variety of birds such as hoopoe, Asian blue fairy, jungle myna and pied robin who kept darting in-out of their well camouflaged nests. When friends wanted to know how we achieved this superior quality road construction, we always directed them to Jeeves who could not stop blushing on receiving their well-deserved compliments.

Chapter 60

Pizza Oven

Now that the match was nearly over, it was time to relax.

But Madam wanted one more last minute addition. Having watched the political parties spar with each other to get any bill passed in the Parliament and then finally agreeing when each party gets their favourite bill also listed, I decided to use this tactic. If she wanted an addition, I should also ask for one!

The idea of running an organic cooking class had not just fallen out of the sky, although the solar part of it had. The wife on one of her numerous world tours had attended an organic cooking class in Tuscany and had been very impressed with it. I, of course, was the guinea pig and had my fill of Italian food soon after her return as she wanted to tweak her recently learnt recipes to suit the Indian palate.

Now that she was going to run a cooking class in her own kitchen, she wanted to have a bit of Tuscany in her garden and what better tribute to Italy than a fully operational pizza oven.

The only hitch was finding an expert who could build a good functional wood burning pizza oven.

Unfortunately, the Bangladesh stalwarts had never heard of pizza before and so there was no way they could be assigned with this job.

Jeeves would not have been of any help as his road contractor knew only about the multilayer thickness of road building.

The wood saw mill owner in Kotagiri would have been the ideal person to tap as he also ran a bakery where there were ovens to bake fresh bread. Unfortunately, since we had not given him the contract to cut the shipboard wood but instead bought our own sawing cum planing machine, he may not be that favourably inclined to part with information.

So back to the ex-NPA team and the internet.

Nowadays, all information is freely available on the internet and our architect was more than happy to try his hand at pizza oven building after his success with the fireplace. He was able to download all the information required and then dumbed it down step by step, similar to what the USA TV news producers do, so that even a fifth class fail would be able to follow the instructions.

It was hilarious to watch the mason (fifth class fail) instruct his helper (fifth class pass) to hold up the sheets of drawings in sequence so that he could move forward step by step without missing a beat. The fifth class duo were able to get some of their doubts cleared by the contractor, who by now after having been on the fireplace constructing team, was quite confident that building a pizza oven should be a piece of cake. He was quite right and the pizza oven was later also used to bake cakes.

Since we had followed the parliamentary guidelines in granting both parties their wish list, it was my turn now and my choice was honey.

Not honey – a sweetheart, but honey – from the bees.

Since the garden had a variety of flowers such as geranium, hollyhock, dahlia, roses, etc. I figured having a couple of bee boxes would get us enough honey to fulfill my cravings. I had even located a bee keeper who was willing to set up the boxes and get us a queen bee from the forest and oversee the colony formation. He said in a matter of a month we should be able to get our first batch of home grown honey.

I was eagerly looking forward to getting pure Raven's Nest honey and not being dependent on the glycerin supplemented commercial honey available in most shops.

All was going well, until one early morning we were woken up in Mumbai by a frantic call from the cook at Raven's Nest informing us that a bear had come during the night and knocked down all the boxes and the bees had escaped and were flying wild. I was not worried about the bees but more worried about knowing whether the bear had injured anyone.

Fortunately, all were safe and the bear had left after having its fill of honey and proving that where there is honey, a bear won't be too far behind!

I had to either junk my honey project or shift it to another location which was bear proof. I decided to move it into the organic vegetable garden and build an iron cage around the bee box to keep the bears out.

It's ironical that in a farm, a cage is built to keep the bear out whereas in a city zoo a cage is built to keep the bear in.

Chapter 61
Mosaic Masterpiece

At last we had reached the finish line and I could put my feet up and enjoy a drink. But I could see that the wife was unhappy.

I think all the running around to get the various interior components, chasing the staff to get the work done and thinking on her feet with no support from any corner, had finally taken its toll.

She just sank in the sofa and announced, "I am fed up with this house and if someone agrees to buy it at the right price, I want to sell it!"

Wow that was a shocker and I sure hope she didn't really mean it! After all the effort put into building this fabulous house, I definitely didn't want this to be the final outcome.

I got a little philosophical and told the wife, "Just look at all the different pieces of the jigsaw that have gone into forming this mosaic masterpiece. You should think hard before letting it go as it really is a cosmopolitan house."

In reality, we had a small piece of different parts of this country and even the world in our Raven's Nest:

The tea was planted by the British.

The land belonged to the local Badagas tribe.

The name partly from our granddaughter who was an Indo-Brazilian combination and partly from the Canadian Native Indians bird of worship.

The wood from the Philippines via a ship breaking yard in Gujarat.

The bathroom tiles from Jaipur. The roof tiles from Mangalore.

The wire cut bricks from Kerala.

The rain water guttering chains from Chennai.

The bathroom fittings from Coimbatore.

The light fittings and door handles from Mumbai.

The waterfall idea from Lonavala.

The pizza oven from the Italy cooking class connection.

The solar water panels to conserve energy in keeping with the world environment conservation program.

The Nilgiri refrigerator from the Nilgiris.

The fireplace built according to British dimensions.

The paintings adorning the walls from all over the country.

And if you look at the labour, we had people from Mumbai, Bihar, Uttar Pradesh, Karnataka, Bangladesh and last but not least the local crew.

It really was a labour of love.

PART 8

LABOUR

ALTHOUGH LABOUR IS *painful, you got to stick it out.* Raven's Nest had been built with a lot of effort but the wife wanted to give it up.

RRR was to be demolished but due to a Suo Moto stay was still standing and we wanted to save it.

The irony of the situation was striking and as the saying goes 'there is no gain without pain'.

Now we had to plan on how to save RRR before the stay ran out.

Chapter 62

Master Plans

Our plans had to be rock solid as we were facing some formidable opponents. Normally civil court cases drag on and on endlessly as there are numerous appeals and stays in the higher courts. When the case is finally disposed either one party is dead or has lost all interest in the case which has literally lasted a lifetime.

However, the RRR case created some sort of record as it moved from the City Civil court to High Court and then to the Supreme Court in a short span of three years and a verdict was delivered one year later. Even the terrorist Ajmal Kasab's case did not move so fast. Some external guiding hand was in play here and we had no clue. Something similar to Maradona's famous 'Hand of God' goal in the 1986 World Football Cup final between Argentina and Britain.

All we knew was that RRR was located in Prabhadevi which had become a prime property area thanks to its easy connectivity to the airport and suburbs after the construction of the Bandra Worli sea link and our plot was juxtaposed between two big builders who were in possession of the adjoining properties.

One wanted to build a seven star luxury hotel and the other a seven star luxury apartment complex and the only minor impediment was RRR, located right in the middle. Thanks to it, one was denied building permission due to FSI violation on the plot and the other was denied direct access from the main road necessitating a circuitous route through the adjoining slums. Two big builders working in tandem can spell disaster for small fry as was the case here. The big builder's earlier warning, "In the end you will come crawling back to me on all fours begging for mercy" still resonated in our ears.

Good Generals strategise before going to battle so that they have a well thought out game plan which covers all the angles. Our Hero Robin decided that if David has to go to war with Goliath, then he had better have his slingshot ready and working.

Several midnight meetings later a strategy was worked out wherein three thrust areas were identified and these were legal, media and political.

Identifying the three support legs of a stool is fine but what next?

Chapter 63

Committed Lawyer

Since the harsh judgment had already been delivered, it was essential that we find a loophole to extricate ourselves from this precarious situation as nobody else was going to help us. It made sense to find a senior lawyer who would spend time studying the case diligently and guiding us about what needed to be done next.

Numerous lawyers were knocking on our doors as the 'Suo Moto stay' had evoked a lot of interest in the hitherto low profile RRR case. We didn't want to get involved with the bevy of eager lawyers as they reminded us of the ambulance chasers.

In USA there is a group of lawyers known as 'Ambulance Chasers' whom I had the misfortune of meeting following an accident. A relative of ours happened to slip and fall down in a supermarket resulting in a hairline fracture in the arm.

Before we could even reach the emergency room three lawyers were there waiting to sign us up as potential clients to sue the supermarket for negligence

for not keeping the floor dry. Obviously these lawyers camp in the emergency room waiting for clients and occasionally hit pay dirt.

We weren't convinced that the fall had occurred due to a wet floor as it had appeared bone dry to us and it had most likely occurred because our relative was prone to occasional momentary blackouts over the last several years.

When we mentioned this point to the lawyers, they told us not to talk about this medical problem but just go ahead and sue the supermarket as all are covered by insurance meant for such contingencies. They went on to advise us to get insurance coverage for our house too because if any guest had a similar accident while visiting our home, they could sue us – the home owners!

We thanked the 'Ambulance Chasers' for their free advice and got our house insured, but did not help them in collecting their potential jackpot from the supermarket.

Fortunately in India, we have not reached the 'Ambulance Chaser' stage nor did we have to invest in any liability insurance policy for Raven's Nest as we believed that guests in India are more gracious.

In choosing a lawyer, the wife's high flying contacts always helped as we could use them as a sounding board to identify a lawyer who would be a perfect fit for us.

Lists were drawn, names short-listed and friends were contacted to get us a personal introduction to the chosen one. Several midnight meetings later we zeroed on a brilliant lawyer who had time for us and was willing to go the extra mile to find the key to releasing us from what now seemed to be the RRR dungeon.

CHAPTER 64

DUNGEON KEY

OUR LAWYER WAS a man of few words but he had absolute clarity in his thought process and was able to cut through the chase straight to the main point.

In medical school there are two types of students. The studious or brilliant ones who ultimately become physicians and the casual or average ones who take up surgery. The physician types can spend hours discussing all the different theoretical aspects of a patient's illness, different investigations to order, several treatments to offer and finally embark on a path of treatment after having spent several hours discussing the case threadbare. On the other hand, surgeons see a problem, get the relevant facts and are ready to find a path to solve the problem by cutting out the offending lesion in the shortest possible time.

So if our lawyer had gone to medical school, there is no doubt that he would have been a surgeon but since he is a lawyer, I assume we should refer to him as the surgical lawyer.

Our surgical lawyer's answers were always brief and precise and he made it a habit to answer all queries in the shortest possible time. This suited us fine since our situation was fluid and new hare-brained ideas would crop up daily from various members. All these had to be run by the lawyer as Robin believed in democracy, and wanted all to be heard.

Initially, the long queries sent by Robin were answered in a relatively polite manner but after some time the surgical lawyer returned to his cryptic replies and this upset Robin to no end. It was only much later when we got to know the surgical lawyer better that we understood that his mindset was to filter out all the redundant queries and just answer the relevant points and look in the right places for a solution.

The right place for a solution was the RTI (Right to Information Act).

Our surgical lawyer honed in on this and told us to get all the relevant papers pertaining to RRR during the dark hole years of 1980-2005 as he felt this would be the key to unlock the dungeon door.

CHAPTER 65

PENALTY PAPERS

FORTUNATELY FOR THE residents of RRR the Right to Information Act was passed in 2005 and it allowed ordinary citizens to obtain all pertinent government information relating to any issue under the sun. Little did the crooks involved in the construction of RRR ever envisage that twenty years hence the government would facilitate their Pandora's Box being opened by promulgating the RTI.

Acting on our surgical lawyer's advice, the application forms were filled up in triplicate and promptly dispatched to the RTI office. This exercise had to be repeated several times as we wanted to get all the documents related to the construction of RRR and this entailed sending separate queries to various departments and sub divisions.

The waiting period for receiving an RTI reply is one month and if no reply is received by then, one has to move the request to the next level. This was duly done and the wait continued. Just as we were giving up hope and imagining that this RTI Act was only some sort of media hype, a tempo drove into the lane searching for the infamous RRR.

Watching the overflowing tempo enter the compound, reminded me of the 1980's USA advertisement for a coffee known as Brim where the TV commercials had a tag line 'Fill it to the Rim with Brim'. This tempo was stuffed to the rim with the famous RTI papers.

It is easy to say, "Let's get the RTI papers." But when you get a truckload of them and realise they are all poor quality photocopies with several pages of smudges and unreadable handwritten notes in the side columns, you wonder as to how you are going to decipher their contents. This sure stumped Robin and his band of merry men and women.

But there was a group of youngsters who were eager to get their hands dirty and in some way contribute to saving RRR. This helper group was an appendage of Robin's and so far he had not found a role for them that could satisfy their desire to help. But here was a golden opportunity to put them to work. So they were allotted the task of sorting out the papers by year and department, then reading all the papers, making a brief synopsis and finally highlighting any important paragraphs. This was going to be several all-night exercise, but the young helpers were least worried as they were night birds and their life began only after 11pm.

In Kotagiri, life comes to a standstill at 9pm and these night birds would have been the only traffic plying on the deserted roads after 11pm. Of course, they would have had to share the road with the nocturnal bisons who wander from estate to estate chewing the grass and drinking the water. The watering hole in Raven's

Nest was one of their favourite spots until we built a fence to keep them out.

You also don't get to hear stray dogs barking or see them running around as they are the staple diet of the leopards that also come out after dark and roam the estate roads in search of their prey.

The young helpers enthusiastically spent several nights digging into this heap of papers searching for the proverbial needle in the haystack. They were able to discover some hitherto suppressed facts which clearly underscored what we had been saying all along about the RRR construction: that it was carried out with the implicit connivance of all involved and now the hapless residents were made the scapegoats and hung out to dry.

These facts although pertinent for raising the sympathy factor in favour of the residents had no locus standi in a court of law. The key which would legally unlock the dungeon door still eluded everyone and a fresh review of the RTI papers was now undertaken by Robin and his merry men and women.

Unfortunately, this group was much older than the young helpers, so burning the midnight oil was not part of their regular routine as they followed the dictum of early to bed and early to rise. Fortunately, they also enthusiastically got to work and did not consider this as a penalty posting.

In the Armed Services there are some penalty postings where the hardship quotient is much higher. In the Nilgiris there is a Services Staff College located in Wellington where many young officers spend a few years. Most seem to love this posting which is diametrically opposite to the penalty posting and they also seem to fall in love with the surroundings.

This can be gauged by the fact that many ex-service officers have bought property, built houses and settled down in the Nilgiris.

This cosmopolitan crowd adds to the charm of the hill station.

The more the older group dug into the papers, the more frustrated they became as the enormity of the scandal really hit home. They began to realise that all the key players were either dead or sitting pretty at home and only the RRR residents were facing the wrecking ball on their homes.

Just as hope was fading, a paper with vague penalty calculations was dug out from the heap categorised as containing the most illegible and most difficult to decipher stack of papers. There appeared to be something important buried under all these numerical figures and it was decided to get a fresh copy of this particular paper.

So a fresh RTI application was made for these penalty calculation papers and all kept their fingers crossed that this penalty would kickstart our revival campaign and strengthen the legal leg of our three-legged stool strategy.

CHAPTER 66

SENIOR EDITOR

THE SECOND LEG of the stool was Media and who better than the journalistic wife with her literary society connections to get us a foot in this door. She very proudly rattled off the names of various media personalities whom she knew and those for whom she had written. She finally arranged a meeting with a senior editor but it had slipped her mind that he had done his initial schooling in the Nilgiris.

The British loved the Nilgiris and this was reflected in the lovely, old style British houses built amidst the lush tea gardens and the numerous schools patterned after the famous British Public schools. In the colonial times students in these public schools were British as some of these schools were established over one hundred and fifty years ago. But as time went by, these schools gained national recognition as being prestigious boarding schools and parents from all over the county vied to get their children admission in any one of the Nilgiri schools. However, in my mind I still favour Lawrence School, Lovedale; but you may count my opinion as biased.

There was a fierce rivalry between students from these various public schools on the playing fields, sports arena or debating competitions and each school would aim to run the other down whenever the opportunity arose.

However, now when you meet a person forty years later and he says that he studied in the Nilgiris, old school rivalries are forgotten and eyes light up and an immediate bond is established.

Editors are a different breed and by reputation supposed to be cantankerous, snobbish and have a superiority complex about their intellectual prowess which makes them believe that they are above all ordinary mortals. We were apprehensive while waiting, in the coffee shop, for this hotshot editor to arrive and I could see that the wife in spite of all her bluster was not as relaxed as she normally would have been.

After the initial introductions, the meeting did start in a very formal manner and the editor didn't seem to be very interested in our plight and kept gazing all around the coffee shop giving us the impression that he wanted to get out of there as fast as he could. Suddenly the editor's cell phone rang and very sheepishly, he apologised for having forgotten to turn off his phone and came up with an uncalled for explanation that it was a call from some old school friend from the Nilgiris who was passing through Mumbai.

My antenna immediately picked this up and I quickly mentioned to him that I had also gone to school in Nilgiris and asked him details about his schooling years. One could see the ice immediately melt, and we were on a completely different wicket after that; thanks to the Nilgiris schooling connection. It was one of those fortunate coincidences that this particular friend called up at that particular moment and I felt confident that he would go out of his way to help us.

After giving us a patient hearing and understanding the problem thoroughly, he promised to assign a senior reporter to follow this story but warned us that the story would only move forward if it took on a life of its own and that there was no way he can keep on carrying this story if it got to be boring as then it would die a natural death.

This was a very fair deal and we felt the pendulum was shifting in our favour as he very easily could have washed his hands off our problem and told us that it would not interest any of his readers. We would then have had to go back to the drawing board and search for the next editor to pitch our story.

Reminded me of doctors who send their scientific manuscripts to journals for publication only to get them either rejected or sent back with queries. The latter is good as once the queries are answered satisfactorily, the manuscript is invariably printed. The former is bad as then you have to submit it to another journal whose format and style may be quite different. I suppose authors of fiction novels also face a similar dilemma.

Now that the editor had partially opened the door for us, we were sure that we did not need any spin doctor to help as this was a genuine story with a human angle and the public would identify with it.

Chapter 67
Media Frenzy

As promised, a senior reporter did visit us and we could discern from her demeanor that she was not too enthusiastic about wasting her time in RRR and was only there at the behest of her editor. After getting a few cursory facts, she decamped saying that she had all the information she needed and that we should look out for the article in the next day's newspaper.

We apprehensively opened the newspaper the next day as we were sure that she had not got all her facts right in that short span of time she had spent listening to our woes nor had she really delved into the subject. Sure enough there was a very superficial article written and the most worrying aspect was that she had referred to RRR as an 'upmarket' housing society several times. This word 'upmarket' was bound to lower the sympathy factor amongst the reading public and the casual attitude of the reporter did not augur well for RRR.

As a cancer surgeon, I've always felt that an element of luck (destiny) plays an important role in the final outcome of each individual patient. Two patients may

have a similar disease and the same surgery is done for both. However, one of them may do very well and live for several years while the other may die in a short period of time. Nobody can predict which path either of them will take and it all boils down to the inexplicable destiny quotient.

Similarly, our luck quotient seemed to be strong as the editor called up the next day to apologise saying that the senior reporter he had assigned to our story had to leave unexpectedly due to a sudden illness in her family and he could now only spare a rookie journalist for our story. This seemed to be heaven sent and one of our religious neighbours quoted a biblical phrase "The Lord works in mysterious ways" and was convinced that our luck would change. In fact, this phrase does not appear in the Bible but is a quote of a popular hymn written by William Cooper in 1773; but we were not going to puncture our religious friend's firm belief.

Our luck did change since this rookie journalist really dug into the problem as she wanted to impress her boss with her investigative reporting skills and soon her articles started appearing in the paper. We were pleased to find that the 'upmarket' tag had been dropped as she had realised after actually visiting some of the un-renovated 600 square foot apartments, built in the 1980's, that were anything but 'upmarket'!

During the construction of RRR, these people had been paying the builder in installments, slab by slab and this was the first building built in the complex. The irony was that these people proudly moved into their flats after the builder boasted that he was the first to complete a building in the complex and the Occupation Certificate (OC) would be obtained when the rest of the builders finished their work. There was no way that these innocent buyers could predict that the other five buildings coming up in the complex which would be completed a few years after they moved into their new homes, would consume extra FSI and make their flats illegal.

This sequence of events in fact contradicts the widespread notion put out by the authorities that all those who bought flats in RRR were well aware that the whole building complex was illegal. I am sure the occupants of this first constructed building would never have been able to foresee what was going to happen when the other buildings came up several years later even if they had consulted Nostradamus!

Once the plight of these innocent buyers was highlighted in graphic detail by the rookie reporter, the story started taking a life of its own. It moved from a small column in the middle pages to a large column on the front page and started attracting more media attention.

Once the print media gets involved, the TV crew can't be far behind and gradually the parking lot of RRR seemed to have more TV vans than residents' cars. The media coverage did reach a crescendo the day the bulldozers came to break the gates and live TV updates were constantly flowing out of RRR screaming 'Breaking News' every fifteen minutes. The newspaper headlines also got bigger and bolder with numerous gut-wrenching photos of women clinging to the gates hoping to prevent the bulldozers from moving forward. These images were circulated around the nation and ultimately resulted in the famous 'Suo Moto Stay'.

The wife on one of her shopping trips to Coonoor was stopped in front of the herbal oil shop by a stranger who excitedly proclaimed, "Haven't I seen you on TV

resisting the bulldozers at RRR and on an evening talk show?" Very soon a small curious crowd gathered around the celebrity wife and all expressed their admiration for what she was doing and the fight being put up by the RRR residents.

The unanimous public opinion in that small excited crowd was that the builders and authorities who had committed the crime should be punished and not the residents. The wife was very happy with her new found glory and the public support for RRR even in a small town so far away from Mumbai.

The owner of the herbal store was so pleased that a celebrity had entered his shop and had brought along a number of excited new clients that he insisted on giving her a discount, proving once again that the media can influence public opinion.

Thanks to the media, RRR became a household name and the daily developments were being followed minutely all over the country. Well, actually our rookie reporter and her Nilgiri school educated editor were the ones who set the ball rolling and now the story just kept spiralling down the hill, gathering momentum as it went along.

CHAPTER 68

POLITICAL BIGWIGS

THE POLITICAL LEG was the last but most important leg of the stool. This proved to be a stumbling block as none of us were politically connected nor had had any occasion to interact with politicians. A law abiding citizen generally does not have to deal with politicians and the universal perception is that all politicians are crooks and will only help you if there is something in it for them. But the whole RRR experience dramatically changed this perception a full hundred and eighty degrees.

Since we did not have any political contacts, we had no clue as to where to begin. We spoke to some friends who knew some business people who had dealt with politicians in the past. Their feedback was very worrisome as they said nothing moves without money and no politician will meet you without large sums of money being deposited with his or her agent.

Thus, we were in an impossible situation as our coffers were nearly dry and Al Capone along with his dirty dozen still refused to pay their share of the legal dues. But Al Capone was enamoured by the media and loved to strut in front of all the TV cameras and make out as though he was the leader of the RRR campaign. The true colours of a person always come to the fore in times of crisis and if Al Capone adorned the negative side of the coin, the slew of politicians we met, competed amongst themselves to adorn the positive side of the coin, without expecting anything in return.

The State Government has all the powers to change the rules and if there is a political will a way can be found out of any tight situation. Unfortunately, most State Governments are remote-controlled by the powers that be in Delhi. We were told that if an order comes from Delhi, all local barriers would be lifted and RRR would be saved. So we had taken a full circle and come back to the starting point as we did not have the money to get this high command audience in Delhi.

But like the 2009 Bollywood movie 'Luck by Chance', we got an unexpected break. A patient of mine who owned a pizza restaurant came for his regular follow up and since I was not too busy that day we spent a few extra minutes discussing RRR as he had read about it in the papers. He happened to ask me if he could be of any use and I jokingly said, "Yes if you can give me tons of money." He asked me why I needed the money and when I mentioned it was for arranging a high level meeting in Delhi, he just laughed and said, "Doc, you don't need any money. I will arrange the meeting for you!" Of course I did not believe him then but when he called a few days later and asked me to visit his office to finalise the dates for the meeting, I felt it was time to share this information with the rest of the gang.

Robin and his merry men and women were totally skeptical of this new adventure as they had been told that without money nothing works in Delhi and there is no way you can get an appointment for free. They were even more skeptical when I told them that the meeting had been arranged by the pizza man and it would be a good idea if all of us went and met him. But just to humour me they came along to meet the pizza man who, unknown to me, was actually working in tandem with a very gracious politician.

To cut a long story short, the pizza man arranged the meeting, the gracious politician accompanied us to Delhi, we did get a relaxed meeting with the high command and no money was paid!

Someone was looking out for RRR.

But in view of the harsh Supreme Court judgment, the government in power was not keen on helping us in spite of their good intentions and the nudge from Delhi.

Chapter 69

Political Unity

If the government in power cannot help us, what about the opposition?

Now that we were all over the media thanks to the 'Suo Moto Stay', we were welcomed with open arms by all the opposition politicians. Merely announcing that we were the RRR group was enough and all were keen to express genuine concern and extend a helping hand.

It was an eye opener to see how all the political parties went out of their way to make us feel at home in their respective offices, made sure we were well fed, listened patiently to our grievances and then tried to work out some strategy to help us and also arrange for meetings with their party's big bosses. Many of them from different parts of the city came to RRR to express their solidarity with our cause and this helped tremendously in boosting our morale as it is only in adversity that you realise who your true friends are.

Surprisingly, all this was done without expecting anything in return. We did not have any money to offer nor we were a large vote bank and in many instances did not even belong to the politician's district. When we narrated this to our friends, all were as surprised as us. Our collective impression of politicians took a complete U-turn and we came to appreciate the long hours and hard work they put in with the sole purpose of helping the public. We pledged that come next election all of RRR will make it a point to vote and also urged all our friends to vote as the political class needs to be strengthened.

All the opposition parties pledged to help us and raise the issue in the assembly. This must have been the only assembly session where all the parties, ruling and opposition, were on the same page with the sole intent of helping the residents of RRR. No fireworks in the assembly only genuine suggestions put forward to find a solution.

The press was also quite surprised with the camaraderie displayed among all politicians when the RRR topic was brought up and were curious to know what magic we had worked to get all on our side. We had a hard time convincing them that there was no magic and it was only thanks to the integrity of the media that our plight had found sympathetic visibility. Now the politicians were getting interested because they had realised that it was a gigantic problem wherein for the first time in independent India, law abiding, taxpaying citizens were getting the short end of the stick and were living in fear of the potential loss of their homes along with their life savings.

However, with the harsh Supreme Court judgment hanging over the issue, it appeared that there was no way forward. But now with all three legs of the stool in place, it was time to take the fight to the enemies' camp. Forward ho you Merry Men!

PART 9

BIRTH

BIRTH IS A *miracle and all pray for a healthy child.*
Here we had two children: the healthy Raven's nest and the unhealthy RRR. Only a miracle could save RRR.

Chapter 70

White Knight

It is often said that miracles do happen and fortune favours the brave. This is exactly what transpired in the never ending RRR saga. A white knight who did not live in Mumbai and had no connection with RRR but had closely followed our battle in the press, appeared out of the blue and took it upon himself to plunge into the fight to save RRR. By this time all three legs of our strategic stool were in overdrive.

The print media kept plugging away unearthing different facets of the sordid story. RRR was on prime time news and members from the compound were invited to join the evening shouting talk show programs. These talk shows apparently are widely watched around the country as was evident by the wife being recognised and given celebrity status outside the herbal oil shop in Coonoor. The highly visible hoardings around the city carried various messages on RRR. Even those who were initially reluctant to associate with RRR were soon ardent supporters when they realised this was gaining national attention and their banners on Marine Drive would attract more eyeballs if they highlighted the RRR plight.

The political class cutting across party lines was actively working both behind the scenes to find a solution and also in front of the cameras giving sound bites supporting the residents of RRR.

The legal team was studying the RTI papers, especially the penalty calculations garnered from the smudged RTI papers to shore up the defense strategy.

The white knight brought himself up to speed with all these three different thrust areas and then said that he was going to present the facts to an altruistic Supreme Court lawyer and if she was convinced with the genuineness of the case, he was certain she would take up the cause and fight tooth and nail to extricate RRR from this doomed position.

Chapter 71

Altruistic Lawyer

The altruistic Supreme Court lawyer spent several hours, literally burning the midnight oil, reading the whole case thoroughly from cover to cover and after being convinced that something was amiss, willingly agreed to take up the case.

The medical profession which is supposed to be altruistic, is fast gaining notoriety as being money minded. This is highlighted regularly with articles in the press about doctors being sent on travel jaunts by pharmaceutical companies with the hope that their drugs will be prescribed. Not to be outdone, a high end hospital in the Mumbai suburbs was hauled up by the Medical Council for sending referral fees back to the family doctors whose patients underwent surgery at this facility. Referral fees are a sophisticated substitute phrase for a 'kickback' and it is totally unethical for a hospital to follow such practices. But unfortunately these hospitals are owned by big industrial houses and they feel medicine is a money-making business.

Fortunately, in my alma mater Christian Medical College, Vellore, the ethics of medicine are still instilled

into every young doctor and they are advised to wear the CMC blinkers when they leave and continue to practice ethical medicine.

Blinkers akin to what Robin wore when he took on the task of saving RRR by concentrating wholeheartedly on it and ethical practice as highlighted by the altruistic Supreme Court lawyer who took up the case not for financial gains but as she was convinced that it was a genuine case where an injustice needed to be corrected.

She filed numerous motions in the Supreme Court requesting for the case to be re-opened in light of the new evidence of penalties having been paid way back in the 1980's for the excess construction done, which had totally been overlooked all these years. If these penalty calculations were accurate, then there was less than ten percent of the construction that could be deemed illegal as opposed to sixty percent now slated for demolition. A huge difference by any stretch of the imagination.

CHAPTER 72

ELECTRIC DISCONNECTION

IMAGINE THE UPPER thirteen floors of an eighteen storey building being demolished and the lower five floors being left undisturbed and preserved in such a manner that they are habitable. This was the tender floated by the authorities as they had to comply with the Supreme Court order.

An expert demolition company that had done similar work for the corporation was finally chosen. When contacted on phone, they told the authorities that there should be no problem in slicing off the upper thirteen floors using imported laser technology or at the very least puncturing the walls to make the place uninhabitable.

However, after a site visit their attitude changed completely and they sent frantic messages to Robin for a private meeting. Private meetings are always suspect as the agenda is unknown and after several personal calls Robin with a few of his merry gang, very reluctantly agreed, as they were clutching at all straws.

To their utter surprise the meeting turned out to be very positive as the demolition man said that he had happily applied for the job as this was a high paying one very much in line with his business. But only after visiting the site did he realise that the building was actually occupied and this job entailed breaking people's homes and rendering them homeless. His religion did not permit this and he could not live with this guilt for the rest of his life, so he was turning down the job. He was quite willing to get blacklisted for future contracts but would not go against his religious beliefs. This was God sent.

Since the residents refused to vacate the buildings on their own accord, the government decided to smoke them out by cutting off the municipal water, gas connections and electric supply. This did not cause too much heart burn as lack of municipal water was the root cause which drew us to court and led to this cascading effect. So by technically cutting off the municipal water supply, nothing much had changed.

Gas connections were also easily cut but a more environment friendly medium for cooking was found.

The wife led the way in demonstrating the Raven's Nest philosophy of using solar cookers on the terrace. Hopefully she may be able to recruit some new customers for her solar, organic cooking class in the Nilgiris.

Electricity was another matter, as the wires were all arranged haphazardly in the meter room and the services of the local electricians had to be enlisted to complete the task. Once cut, the lifts were shutdown and this made all of us physically fitter as we had to use the stairs. Individual TVs did not work, so we spent more time in the lobby gathered around the common building TV bonding with neighbours; something that nobody does in Mumbai as all are busy locked up in their small cocoons with no time for relatives let alone neighbours.

Like the Chinese labour who helped build Lawrence School in the 1850's and left their Chinese money in the form of tokens to be used for buying sweets in the tuck shop, Mumbai is now flooded with Chinese products which are cheaper than their Indian counterparts and result in Indian tokens flowing back to China.

Chinese crackers burn away during Diwali and light up the Mumbai sky. Similarly, our dark homes were lit up by Chinese battery operated, rechargeable lamps. These lamps were left in the lobby every morning to charge and in the evenings burnt bright in our houses. Anyone looking up from the road would imagine that the electricity had not been cut as these lights were pretty dazzling.

In fact some enthusiastic newspaper reporters with their photographers in tow paid us a surprise visit one evening as somebody from the road must have told them that the lights were burning bright in most of the upper flats. To their utter shock they realised that these were in fact battery-operated lights and once switched off resulted in total darkness.

They left convinced that the Supreme Court orders were being followed but being sympathetic to the residents' plight kept reassuring us that it is always darkest before dawn and that we should just hang in there. They may have said this to boost our morale, but their words were so prophetic as our altruistic Supreme Court lawyer was able to get her foot in the door and convince the learned judges to listen to her recently uncovered RTI facts.

The Supreme Court by now had realiszed that the initial order may have been right in the legal sense but was unjust in a moral sense especially with these new

RTI skeletons regarding the penalties paid tumbling out. The Supreme Court was willing to send the case back to the State Government for redressal. Since the elections had just resulted in an upheaval and the new State Government was willing to help, the Supreme Court had no hesitation in washing its hands off the case and returning it to the State to sort out legally.

Another God sent miracle had happened in RRR. The Supreme Court had removed the shackles; thanks to the penalties and the residents could breathe easy.

CHAPTER 73

SILVER LINING

THE PENALTY CLAUSE had unshackled RRR from the clutches of the Supreme Court and the present Government was looking at all the legal avenues to save RRR.

However, several years of fighting the RRR battle had taken its toll. All had lost money. Many had to pawn their jewellery to pay for their own expenses and those of the other nonpaying variety.

Some had left at the first sight of the bulldozers and rented small flats in other buildings. Many of them had to rent in the suburbs as the buildings surrounding RRR had jacked up their rents anticipating brisk business. When the bulldozers were pulled back due to the various stays, they could not return to their own flats as they had signed one year leases in their new rented places. So these poor folk had to commute great distances as their place of work was near RRR, while keeping their flats in RRR locked or reoccupying them but continuing to pay the rent on their recently leased flats. This sure was a double whammy.

A few elderly residents developed high blood pressure, a few had strokes and some even died. The stress got to everyone and some marriages also fell apart.

However, every cloud has a silver lining and this saga sure had a few of them.

Since all were fighting a common cause and spending sleepless nights strategising how to solve the problem, several late night meetings were held. These were followed by late night coffee breaks where one actually got to know who lived in the compound. New acquaintances were made and lifelong friendship bonds were established.

We learned that the political class was not always rotten and heartless as we saw the other side when we met several of them and found them to be genuinely moved by our plight and going all out to help us irrespective of their political affiliations.

The power of the media was appreciated as they were instrumental in making RRR a household name in all the four corners of this country and even abroad. But more importantly, the media coverage got the general public to become aware of the importance of an OC and the perils of entering a building which does not have the proper documentation in place.

Finally, this was instrumental in nudging the Government to pass a bill in Parliament, which was supported by all parties, to protect innocent home buyers so that there would be no repeat of the RRR saga in future.

Part 10

Infancy

An early but important phase in the development of a child or a project.

Chapter 74

Unwanted Visitor

WHILE RRR WAS waiting for the State Government to find a solution, Raven's Nest was facing the fallout of another government.

One evening while the wife was sipping her evening tea and reading an interesting novel, she had an uninvited visitor who happily drove up the fully tarred driveway and announced that he wanted a room. Fortunately, the commercial electricity connections were not functional so the homestay portion of the house was not operational. Our uninvited visitor left saying that when he visited again in the following year he would love to stay here as by then he hoped that we would be fully operational.

The wife was pleased that she had now received her first potential guest for the following year but was a bit nervous as this person had driven in with two flunkies in a car which bore a flag, obviously representing some political party. Not being interested in local politics, she was least interested in finding out about his political affiliations.

The mix of people living in the Nilgiris besides being cosmopolitan are very friendly. They love visiting their neighbours unlike the cocoon mentality of the Mumbai flat owners. One of our nearest neighbours who also ran a very successful homestay happened to visit the wife a few days later. When she narrated the incident of the uninvited visitor, he immediately warned her.

It seems when the lady political honcho visits the Nilgiris, all her feet prostrating flunkies follow and invade all the surrounding homestays. They trash the homestays as their main aim of getting away from their families is to drink, eat like gluttons and not bother about what they break. In fact this neighbour reported that he had some lovely jacuzzis installed in his homestay which were broken after one such drunken brawl. They did not even have the courtesy to ask for a bill as they thought that it was their birthright to stay free and the length of stay depended on how long their Madam remained in the hills. An unlucky homestay owner who had the misfortune of being invaded by this uncouth group of flunkies for a month was on the verge of closing his business as he ran up big losses.

On hearing this unnerving firsthand report, the wife's plans of opening a homestay evaporated! Why be burdened with the hassle of putting up with such a crowd and how was one to control this sitting in Mumbai? After all the hard work put in to make this a top class house, the last thing she wanted was to see the place trashed.

Dejected, she narrated this episode to our lawyer the next day and told him that her plans of opening a homestay had been shelved. He immediately told her to calm down, take a deep breath and transfer the headache to him. He told her the simple solution to this problem was to find a person who would screen all the guests and politely but firmly keep the unwanted riffraff out.

He knew the right person for this job. She was a dynamic lady who was very well respected in the area and had vast experience in the hospitality industry.

The dynamic lady met the wife a few days later and the wife who was depressed with the thought of her homestay plan going up in smoke immediately perked up as this lady fit the bill to a T. She was charming, experienced, willing to take up the job but at the same time had enough clout to run a tight ship. She categorically told the wife to relax in Mumbai and leave all the local running around and managing of the property to her.

Thanks to the uninvited political visitor, the wife got to know about the pitfalls of running a homestay. The wife had bypassed this mine-field before it was too late by finding the right person to take the load off her shoulders and her homestay plans remained on track.

CHAPTER 75

DYNAMIC LADY

THE DYNAMIC LADY also managed three other homestays in the Nilgiris and so was well aware of all the permissions to be obtained. As alluded to earlier, getting the necessary permissions is like running the marathon with hundreds of road blocks along the way. Quite unlike in the other parts of the country where homestays are welcomed and the government goes out of its way to encourage them.

Many flat owners in Mumbai rent out bedrooms in their flats under the loose terminology of homestay. Not many permissions are required other than a green signal from their respective housing societies. This is a win-win situation for the visitor and home owner. Many State Governments having realised this and are giving tax incentives to open new homestays. But this is not the case in the Nilgiris as the hotel owners feel that their business is being affected and the strong hotel lobby has tried its best to erect obstacles through their friends in the Government.

The local authorities themselves are not clear on what permissions are required and can send one on a wild goose chase. However, since our dynamic lady was well-versed in this department, she took it upon herself to educate them.

An unheard of certificate for the building stability was easy to obtain as our property was extra stable in view of the prolonged curing it had undergone. Additionally, the person authorised to give this certificate was our contractor's brother and obviously he was not going to certify his own brother's work as unstable!

A firefighting certificate was another requirement. This sounded absurd as most houses in India are built with solid concrete and house fires are rare.

While living in USA, we were accustomed to hearing the distinct sound of fire engine sirens at all unearthly hours. Home fires occurred quite frequently there as wood was used in constructing the houses and many were prefabricated.

In Raven's Nest, we had used a large quantity of seasoned wood from the ship for the flooring and were keen to comply with the firefighting requirements. As a matter of fact, we had installed extra firefighting extinguishers in the premises. When we insisted on the firefighting chief visiting the house and thoroughly checking out the firefighting equipment, he was quite shocked as most home owners were happy if he just shared a cup of tea with them and after a cursory glance gave them the certificate.

The commercial tax certificate was most difficult to obtain as there was only one commercial tax officer in the Nilgiris and he had to cover the whole district. Our dynamic lady spent a fair amount of time chasing the elusive tax officer around the Nilgiris as he would be visiting different towns daily. She seemed to enjoy this chase as she was addicted to HILL driving!

The tax certificate is essential before any homestay starts operations. But most in Nilgiris give this a wide berth as they prefer cash transactions and can avoid these taxing times. But after having seen what went on in RRR and the power of RTI to unearth documents several decades later, we were keen to go by the book.

Chapter 76

Guest Feedback

Fortunately, no RTI was required to start a homestay. Our dynamic lady got all the necessary permissions in record time and Raven's Nest was ready to open its doors for business.

In keeping with the cosmopolitan nature of the Nilgiris, the staff also came from different parts of the country and were from different ethnic backgrounds. Our cook was from deep-south Tamil Nadu, house help from Nainital, gardener from Karnataka, driver from the local indigenous tribe, maid from Ooty and garden helpers from the local village. They were all very sincere, hard workers but had a major communication problem amongst themselves as all spoke different languages and ultimately the common mode of communication was Pidgin English!

The initial trickle of guests in Raven's Nest had to put up with teething problems as the staff was still not geared up to handle them. But with the dynamic lady keeping a close watch and correcting their shortcomings, the early wrinkles got ironed out.

Once the reviews from satisfied guests started appearing on popular travel websites, the trickle turned into a torrent. There was universal praise for the excellent interior work and attention to detail. The wife lapped up these accolades as she had put in a tremendous effort to achieve this.

Her other goal for running a homestay was to interact with a cross section of people and this too seemed to be falling into place as guests came from all over the country.

There was a doctor family from Gujarat who were avid bird watchers and enjoyed themselves walking amongst the tea bushes photographing different varieties of birds. They were able to distinguish nineteen different species of birds including the Asian pied starling, Bushchat, Red vent bulbul and the ever present Raven! They sent back a detailed photo album with the suggestion that the wife should buy a high-powered binoculars and include bird watching as one of the attractions in Raven's Nest.

Another architect couple from Bangalore was so smitten with the place that they said that as architects they could not find one single shortcoming in this place and returned thrice with different members of their family.

A real estate tycoon from Delhi fell in love with the place, extended his stay by two days and told the wife to start looking out for some property which he could buy. Although, having recently gained practical experience, she was definitely not going to volunteer her services for the interior work!

A renowned hotelier from Mahabaleswar was so enamoured with the overall charm of the house that she made intricate notes and drawings so that she could incorporate some of these features in her well established hundred bed hotel there.

Interacting with such a variety of people and listening to their lavish praise of Raven's Nest raised the wife's self-esteem and now she was at peace with herself, finally having realised that she had created a masterpiece. This was a welcome change after having had some doubts and even gone to the extent of entertaining thoughts of selling the place.

She finally decided to spend more time in Raven's Nest as she felt the cosmopolitan crowd in the Nilgiris was more sincere than her high society group in Mumbai. People here seemed more content with life, having built their dream houses amongst the luscious tea gardens and were not busy trying to pull each other down while competing in a rat race as happens in Mumbai.

She spent her time reading, watching the tea grow, planning for her solar cooking class and socialising with the guests who continued praising the excellent set up she had established. Soon she realised, life was getting a bit dull.

So what next? Maybe start another homestay in Kotagiri as she was an experienced hand now!

She had come to appreciate that, besides being a source of gainful employment to several people, a homestay really enhances the popularity of the region and encourages tourists from different parts of the country to spread the word around amongst their friends, if their own experience in the homestay had been enjoyable.

From the feedback she had received so far, Raven's Nest definitely fulfilled these criteria. She was confident that if the Government here was half as helpful as that in other parts of the country, homestays would definitely play a major role in boosting tourism in the Nilgiris.

Just about this time a doctor family from Chennai came to visit and after hearing about the trials and tribulations she had gone through to build this homestay, encouraged her to write about it saying others around the country would also find it very interesting. Like a prisoner who is allowed a last wish before going to the gallows, this doctor family suddenly jumped out of their car just as they were exiting the big black gates of Raven's Nest and appealed with folded hands to the wife to fulfill their last request.

It was a brilliant idea, full of potential. But perhaps, because of a writer's block or because her mind was cluttered with plans to open her next homestay, she put this on the back burner. Thus, giving me an opportunity to jump into the fray and throw my hat in the literary arena.

This was the beginning of the long arduous homestay journey that finally ended in a slight role reversal. The wife became a coy, homebound lady interested in taking care of her numerous guests and me a pompous writer strutting around the house with grandiose plans of attending the next literary festival either in Jaipur or Ooty!

While RRR remains in suspended animation waiting for a legal loophole to squeeze through, Raven's Nest continues to grow in popularity attracting people from all over India.

The wife's new venture with a French sounding name 'Chalet Mon Ami' to entice the international traveller is in its infancy and I am seriously contemplating a career change. Planning to move from cutting up people to writing about people after having successfully guided you through this adventure.

However, one must not lose focus on how this journey began:

The mountains beckoned and Raven's Nest was born.

The wife beckoned and Chalet Mon Ami was born.

I beckoned and a writer was born.

Hold on a second, I better sign off now before I become delusional and transform myself from a literary novice to a literary icon and start writing about the new home stay, Chalet Mon Ami!

In keeping with its French name, *au revoir* my friends, till we meet again!

ACKNOWLEDGMENTS

TO MY LATE parents who enrolled me in Lawrence School, Lovedale at the tender age of six enabling me to develop a love for the Nilgiris which is the cornerstone of the existence of Raven's Nest and the birth of this story.

To my dear friend, the late Jeya Thilaka Chellam, who helped us at every step from acquiring the land to advising us at different stages of the journey.

To the Dr. Sethupathi Family, for having planted the idea of writing this story in our head. To Madhavi, Sriram, Firdaus, Shireen, Fabricio, Markos, Nalini, Namrata and Alka for their succinct comments. To Margaret Joseph for her dedicated editorial work.

To the publishers, White Falcon Publishing for the professional job done.

My twelve year old granddaughter, Raven, who after reading the first ten pages felt it was a very funny story and encouraged me to continue with this style of writing. Her only grouse being that her grandmother is not like what she has been portrayed.

Raven's grandmother, Vidya (aka my dear wife), the total antithesis of the character in this book who spent all her energy, sweat and effort to make Raven's Nest the beauty it is today. In doing so, she was completely sapped and had no desire to document this adventure.

Thus by default, it fell in my lap and Vidya has washed her hands off the project and told her journalism students to only read this book so as to ascertain how not to write a novel!

DR. V. SRINIVAS is a leading urological cancer and robotic surgeon working at Hinduja hospital and Asian Cancer Institute, Mumbai.

He did his schooling at Lawrence school Lovedale, Nilgiris, undergraduate medical studies at Christian Medical College, Vellore and super specialisation at Memorial Sloan Kettering Cancer Center, New York.

He has published over 100 scientific papers in International medical journals and authored a surgical text book. But, this is his first foray into creative writing.

He was an avid tennis player and an enthusiastic martial arts student in his younger days. However nowadays, while relaxing at Raven's nest, he sticks to watching movies, pottering around the garden (more aptly chasing the gardener!), going for long leisurely walks with his lovely wife and playing a lazy game of tennis before hitting the bar!